RAISING THE GROUND LOWERING THE SKY

Finding Success in a Life Lived Within Mental Illness

A Memoir by Howard Meyer

Dedication

To my parents and my daughter Olivia, for without whom this book would never have been written.

Acknowledgments

To Michael Sklaroff for his invaluable edit on the first draft, to Lisa Fugard, who did an "iron woman" edit leading to the final draft. To Front Line Books for seeing the value in my story and their crack team, Eva Millar and Anna Park, for so skillfully putting the book into print and letting the world know. To Wiley Books, thank you for taking the book into stores worldwide. My cousin Alan Unger, for believing in my artistry before anyone else did. My brother and his hilarious sense of humor. To my entire Axial Theatre/HMActing family, who have been feeding me with soul, spirit, and courage all these years.

To my dear friends Rachel Jones, Lisa Millanazzo, Ryan Mallon, Bret Primack, Stephen Palgon, and Lisa Hertz for holding me up when I had a hard time standing by myself. To all my amazing lifesaving therapists: Carol, Su, Joyce, Dr. Silver, and Susan. To the entire Alanon fellowship and all my Alanon friends, the Buddhadarma, Jesus Christ and his apostles, my Jewish upbringing, and the Religious Society of Friends. Michael Howard, Gabrielle Berberich, Greg Chwerchak, and every single student I have ever taught.
Steve Kirkman, my first artistic running mate, for his inspiration and tireless work editing the audiobook.

And.. Annie Terrazzo, for her incredibly inspirational cover art for the book and her friendship.

My dad liked to pal around with my friends, one of the manifestations of his mental illness. Inappropriate behavior was one of his tells. On this day, before his menacing return, I was embarrassed as I always was by this behavior and the obvious discomfort of my friends. I plucked up my courage and finally said something.

"Dad, let me hang out with my friends."

"You are hanging out with your friends."

"By myself…. Without you here."

Speaking my truth as I entered my teen years, especially about him, always came at great risk. Saying something that evoked his embarrassment, and perhaps his own awareness of his idiosyncratic behavior, could, like it did that day, evoke his wrath. His anger was never instant. He would brood, obsess, sometimes for hours, and then suddenly transform from the joyful, fun, playful father into something quite terrifying. I always braced, assuming a defensive posture, after I finally plucked up enough courage to respond to his odd or rude behavior. Sometimes, he would laugh at my response. Other times, quicksilver, he would strike, sharp, hard, to a body part that was exposed. But never to my face. In that way, this event at the ballfield was entirely unprecedented. If I wasn't protecting myself, vulnerable on the bench top, he would have knocked my head clear off my shoulders. Also, he had never returned to a scene to exact his rage.

I am fourteen years old, sitting on top of the park bench, like all the cool players did, on the visitor's side of the softball field, awaiting my turn at bat. I see my father, Carl, entering the back entrance of the park. I can tell from his body language and determination that he's not in a good mental place- a combination of a black panther and a heat-seeking missile trained on its target. I had developed a laser awareness of all his emotional states, a necessary survival skill.

As he gets closer, I can see his eyes, which are eyes I have seen like these on too many occasions. Deep blue and narrowed with rage, catalyzed by dark, obsessive thinking.

Right before the first fist came crashing down, my arms huddled over as much of me as I could possibly protect, he growls,

"Don't EVER speak to me like that again."

All my friends in the field, who are waiting for me to step into the batter's box, are stuck still, frozen by shock as if any slight movement would bring the same punishment down on them. Likely, not one of them had ever seen anything quite like this- violence masquerading as parental discipline, so public and unhinged. And then, as quickly as he arrived, he left, reversing his path through the back of the park.

I was twelve, and my brother Andrew was seven, on a snowy Queens, New York Sunday. He and I were watching a Minnesota Vikings game (our favorite football team because of the cool uniforms) and engaged in some brotherly roughhousing likely inspired by the football. In an instant, Andrew toppled from my back to the carpet and…. snap, a dreadful sound I can still hear, his arm broken in two. Right before they took him to the hospital, to our disbelief, my dad had to sit down and have a bowl of Carvel soft serve ice cream from the freezer, eating his primary form of self-soothing. Directly after he finished his bowl, he got up from the table, moved into the bedroom where I had retreated, and punched me on the side of my thigh. A dead leg, as we used to call it, causes the entire leg to go numb. After the ice cream and the punch, he was ready to take my brother to the emergency room.

How could the same guy who taught me how to play baseball, took me to every little league game, introduced me to art and nature, and spent hours fishing with me turn on me like this? The everyday reality was almost too much for him to handle, so these difficult moments required more of him than he had to give. And that threshold would shift and change according to his mental state.

Every time I walked home from the same park, from the age of ten (and especially that day), I wondered what awaited me upon my arrival. Would my father be holding on to what had happened a few hours early? Would he have told my mother, and would I find her on the floor knocked out from one of his punches or worse? Would my young brother be hiding under the bed, a place where I took refuge during their fights? Or would it be like nothing at all happened? This was the usual case after an incident like this. Even on days that were normal, in our sense of normal, you never knew what father and mother you'd be walking into. When my dad was depressed, he'd be sleeping, and when he was manic, he'd be singing and dancing.

This was the axis my childhood spun around. Meteorologist of my father's weather. Extreme love could instantly turn into violence.

How did I survive this childhood? How did I manage to come through all this and achieve the success I have— not only live with a father who was finally diagnosed as Schizoid Affective (a nice moniker for Schizophrenia *and* Bipolar disorder), but I was finally diagnosed with Major Depressive disorder and eventually Bipolar as well. I am a playwright who has written over twenty plays, most of which have been produced; I started an acting program in its thirtieth year and a professional theatre in its twenty-fifth. By the end of these pages, I hope to have found that answer.

****

Some twenty years later, already a life-worn thirty-three, I was standing in front of Carl's gravesite at his funeral, dead at 64. I referred to him as my first best friend. I meant it completely. Most would say that he died too young, but in reality, his early demise, to me, was an act of Grace. I wasn't doing very well. Since I left Brandeis University when I was twenty, moved into a dark furnished basement apartment in Queens, and started NYU, I was quite depressed. Since the age of eighteen, when I was diagnosed with a digestive malady that even the conservative gastroenterologist agreed was psychosomatic in nature, I was seeing a therapist or psychiatrist. My stepfather, post gastro- diagnosis, set me up with one of his colleagues' sons in the Boston area in my freshman year at Brandeis. Like my stepdad, he was a strict Freudian. I didn't know it at the time, but that method of therapy would never work for me. When I transferred back to NYU, my stepfather found me another psychiatrist, this time one of his personal colleagues. Also, another Freudian (he had the couch. I sat, but I didn't lie). Both men, the first near Boston and the second a few miles away from where I lived provided insights, care, and great intelligence but more or less kept me afloat during my early and mid-twenties. Progress? Not really sure. It did get me to a place in my late twenties where I needed more, and after a few inquiries, I found Carol, a psychotherapist who paved the path for my deep and sustainable recovery from my childhood. She was steeped in something called Core Energetic therapy, the creators and protégées of Wilhelm Reich, who had developed body-based therapy. The underlying philosophy is that all of our psychological wounds are held in the body, and if carefully and professionally observed, the skilled therapist can ascertain what caused the wounding and, through a combination of talk therapy and body-based techniques, release the pain. This process, which went on for fifteen years, saved my life. I cried rivers and oceans, tears that had been locked up inside of me for thirty-plus years.

But standing next to my father's gravesite, though I presented with dignity and honored my father's passing with love and grief, I was a wreck. I had been a little man from the time of adolescence, and now it was clear that I had no clue how to be a big man. By now, I was deeply depressed, and soon thereafter, I became suicidal. Suicidal ideations, they call them. If you are ever grappling with these feelings and decide to get help, the moment you admit them to any medical practitioner, they have to admit you to a psychiatric ward. Talk to your therapist. Tell them what is going on. See if you can work it out with them. Likely, like me, they will refer you to a psychiatrist who will keep your confidence and prescribe what you need to help those thoughts and feelings lift.

I did just that, and my healing path began in earnest.

By this time in my dad's life, he had been married and divorced for a second time, became unemployable because of his ever-diminishing mental capacity, and spent most of his days as an outpatient at the Mamaroneck, New York campus of St. Vincent's hospital. But that day, all I could remember was seeing the world through the healthy part of my dad. It was a place filled with an infinite number of curiosities and joys. His body stretched itself out inside lakes, oceans, and fields of sport. Healthy dad never met a person he wasn't interested in talking to or flashing his mega-watt smile at. (I have been told that I inherited that smile). He taught me how to stop and see the world.

He loved beauty and loved to draw (He didn't seem to care about the perceived quality; he just enjoyed the process). He had a marvelous Sinatra-Benetesque voice that filled our home regularly. The man was the absolute best hugger. It was a pleasure to be enveloped in one of his bear hugs. I miss those hugs and attempt to replicate them with those I love. He had nothing but joy when I walked into a room to visit him, even in his later diminished years. He was deeply and completely loyal. I got that from him. He was a one-woman man. Another preference I inherited. He valued people, places, sports, food, and experiences. Never things. Money was just a means, never a goal or a badge of success. Time to live— that was his greatest asset and became mine as well.

When I reflect on all the years I was terrified of him, becoming him, running from our similarities, I now can see how model-worthy my dad really was. His quicksilver ferocity scared me. The prospect of inheriting his mental illness turned me averse to his totality. But in my middle years, I began to accept how much we were alike and how substantial a man he was. I even started to see in myself inherited qualities that used to annoy me- his irascibility, his frustration at how people treated each other, his unbridled honesty, which would sometimes drift into the inappropriate, his going on and on, repeating himself when he was imparting his point.

My dad thought I was great, and he told that to anyone who would listen. My aunt, his sister and best friend, tells me that almost every time we speak.

"You and your brother are the best thing I ever did," he would say.

That statement brought a world of pressure, but I knew he meant it. I wish he had been able to see and appreciate all of his own positive qualities, to feel the same way he did about himself as he did about us. His disease prevented it. I am glad he felt that way about us and helped justify his existence to himself. Of course, he needed no justification; none of us do, but in his condition, he needed all the positives he could hang on to. This view offered him solace, and I am grateful for that. As a parent, I absolutely know what he meant and what he felt as a father.

So, there was love and lots of laughs at the root of all the mayhem, violence, and justifiable fear. He was silly and funny—not a tell-a-joke wit and timing kind of guy, but he loved to goof around and laugh. Sometimes at our expense but most often at something innocuous. We posed for a family selfie before selfies were taken by hand, carefully orchestrated with a timer, of the four of us apoplectic with laughter. I wonder what we were laughing at and whatever became of that photo.

****

It is the fall of 1963. I am thirteen months old, and we are on our way to the hospital. My mom, Sarelle, is driving, I'm in a baby seat in the back, and my delirious father is sitting in the front passenger seat. My father was in the middle of his first serious mental breakdown, and my mom, not knowing what was happening to him, was driving him to the emergency room.

This origination story is the foundation for all else that would follow. It was there that my mother learned that my father had a serious case of bipolar disorder, then referred to as manic depression. I have memories of when I was five to six years old, thinking there was something different about my dad. And also about my mother's fickle emotional responses to him. Extremely loving, then hotly judgmental. I came to understand that she was driven by her own terror and her desperate need to control her environment and keep my dad steady. Of course, her sense of control was an illusion. His mental illness was much more powerful than she was. Our mother was just as mercurial towards me and my brother as our dad was. Her rages were as frightening and unexpected, so we learned at a very young age to proceed with both our parents with extreme caution and self-protection. The most acute vigilance was required at home. It was a tinder box. Anything could and did set either of them off.

According to the National Institute for Mental Health, an estimated 2.8% of U.S. adults suffer from bipolar disorder, and the gender split is pretty even. An estimated 4.4% of U.S. adults experience bipolar disorder at some time in their lives. The most disturbing statistic:

"An estimated 82.9% of people with bipolar disorder had a serious impairment, the highest percent serious impairment among mood disorders."

Bipolar disorder, as described by the Substance Abuse and Mental Health Services Administration, is described as "a serious mental illness that causes unusual shifts in mood, ranging from extreme highs (mania or manic episodes) to lows (depression or depressive episodes). A person who has bipolar disorder also experiences changes in their energy, thinking, behavior, and sleep. During bipolar mood episodes, it is difficult to carry out day-to-day tasks, go to work or school, and maintain relationships. Most people are diagnosed with bipolar disorder in their teens or twenties; however, it can occur at any age. People are at a higher risk if they have a family history of bipolar disorder, experienced a traumatic event, and/or misused drugs or alcohol. Differences in brain structure and function may also play a role. When a person has a manic episode, they feel overly excited, productive, and even invincible. On the other hand, when a person has a depressive episode, they feel extremely sad, hopeless, and tired and often suicidal. They may avoid friends and family and may not participate in their usual activities. A severe manic or depressive episode may trigger psychotic symptoms, such as delusions (false beliefs) or hallucinations (seeing or hearing things that others do not see or hear). Bipolar disorder may be treatable with a combination of medication and therapy. Mood stabilizers, antipsychotics, and antidepressants can help manage mood swings and other symptoms."

The tragedy that defined my father's illness was this: according to the National Health Council, 80% of those treated with medicine for bipolar disorder can lead relatively normal, high-functioning lives. My dad fell into the 20% that do not. For him, there was constant medicinal and dose experimentation. Some drugs worked for a while, but all would eventually fail. There were periods when our family had relative peace, and it seemed the doctors had stumbled on a long-term solution.

Part of the failure of his treatment plan was the nascent science of manic depression treatment. This was the 1960s, and an understanding of these more serious mood disorders and psychoses was just being understood. Consequently, he was more of a guinea pig than a patient. He was placed on every new drug introduced to the market that offered some measure of relief from his symptoms. Lithium was the first drug to achieve success and gain traction, and it was finally approved by the FDA in the 1970s. In addition to its inconsistent results, my father experienced various side effects: dry mouth, grizzle at the edge of his lips, emotional numbness, and his big one- weight gain. Because of the inconsistent results, he was given other drugs alongside Lithium as they emerged. Antidepressants- Prozac, Paxil, Lexapro, Zoloft. Anti Anxiety medications- Valium, Xanax, Klonopin. Mood Stabilizers- Depakote, Lamictal, Topomax. These drugs exacerbated all of the above side effects and also added sexual dysfunction, which, at too young an age, he would tell me about and solicit my counsel. What could a nine/ten-year-old offer? Probably more comfort and encouragement than anything else. I would have done and said anything if I thought it could make him feel better.

Some believe that addictive and mental diseases are sentient. That there is actually some kind of consciousness at the center of the state, the literal demons Christ is said to have cast out. If there are sentient demonic forces in the world, this is what they would do to a person- make them feel so hollow, so bad about themselves, so shameful, so useless, that being alive during those phases feels like a ceaseless sentence in a hell realm. After all of that settles down, make them feel so alive, so full of energy, bravado, and unrealistic ambition that they could barely fall asleep. Imagine living a life cycling in and out of all of that with marginal help.

Yet... After all of this, my father would emerge feeling joy and optimism. How was that possible?

To make matters a lot worse, my father also suffered from

schizophrenia, though they didn't know it at the time. Severe manic depression can cause hallucinations. My father had many. One day, he came home and looked at me. He told my mother that I had an antenna coming out of my head and was contacting Mars. At first, we thought he was joking, but we realized he was not. Then came the accusation that my mother was having an affair. He had allegedly overheard the owner of our local hardware store talking about having sex with my mother. Why would he be talking about that with my father in the store? Clearly, this was another hallucination. The most dramatic of these incidents occurred at the height of the Cold War. My schoolteacher father came rushing home from school to announce that the Russians had launched atomic bombs, one headed for New York. He ushered us downstairs to the basement of our three-story apartment building, grabbing as much food as he and my mom could carry. They brought a transistor radio to get updates and instructions from the government. My mother soon wondered why there weren't any other families joining them. She turned on the radio, and there was no news of any attack. It became clear very quickly that this was my dad's confabulation. I always wondered how he felt when the details of these hallucinations were debunked. Did he realize he had just experienced one? Did he acknowledge that he was subject to these convincing voices and images? And my mom- did she hope, every time she drove him to the hospital (there were many such drives), that this time they would have some medicine that would return her life to some semblance of normalcy? Although my dad was prescribed many different drugs, sadly, that day never arrived.

Either schizophrenia or bipolar I would be tragic enough to endure, but to have both. What a life sentence. In Hinduism and Buddhism, there is a strong belief in karma, which refers to the consequences that follow one's actions. Karma can be positive, negative, or neutral and is believed to carry forward from life to life; reincarnation is another pillar of those religions. I have always thought that everyone in my family must have done some really bad shit in previous lives to be born into these circumstances. Despite the trials that the rest of us were forced to endure, my father got the worst of it by far. My brother, my mom, and I went on to live productive lives. My father was never able to. His life was plagued by insurmountable mental and emotional challenges interspersed with fleeting periods of joy. Never any sustained satisfaction.

****

My grandparents, children of immigrants who fled horrible persecution and assault in Russia and Romania, were trained to live within the lines. Stepping outside could present great risks, especially in a new land. Their DNA told them so. They chose respectable careers, married, raised a family, and kept their heads down. My father's progressing condition posed a real problem. If discovered by their communities, they imagined it would bring negative attention and possibly out casting. This fear prevented their own acknowledgment of the early signs of my father's condition. His mother Anne's denial lasted deep into my father's middle years. My only evidence of these indications is through anecdotes relayed by my 92-year-old aunt Rhoda, my father's only living sibling. She spoke of my father as a very sensitive young man who loved to sing. He was extremely handsome and was asked by his peers to sing in their big bands. This culminated when my father, at 21, after college, went to Germany to serve in the peacetime army stationed there. He was almost immediately invited to front the army Big Band. When my dad's service term concluded two years later, he was asked by the army brass to tour other army posts all over Europe. My grandfather Lou, his dad, demanded that he come home. My father, like many immigrant children of that generation, acquiesced. Imagine that. Snatching a dream away from your child. As a parent, I find it impossible to understand. Perhaps a vindictive act relating back to Lou's opportunity to go with Burlington Mills to Philadelphia, which his parents didn't permit. If he couldn't pursue his dreams, he wouldn't permit my dad too. Tragic.

This sensitivity, though a normal characteristic for some, ran much deeper with my dad, I was told. Sensitivity wasn't something accepted by men from certain families in the New York City of that era. Was my grandfather embarrassed and ashamed by his sensitive son? In any case, my dad was chastised ruthlessly by my grandfather… and beaten physically. Being beaten for who you are. Makes me cry just writing that. And someone who was prone to great sensitivity and also bouts of depression. I can only imagine how my grandfather handled my dad's episodes of depression. These imaginary statements ring in my ear: "Buck up, Carl. Pull your pants on and get over it." "No son of mine is going to be a pansy. Toughen up for God's Sake!!!"

My mother received minimal compassion and support from her parents. The same concerns plagued them, I am sure, compounded by my grandmother's severe narcissism. My grandfather was always careful not to rock the boat with his wife. My father's mother Anne's denial turned into blame against my mother. In her mind, it had to be my mother that was driving my father crazy. Terribly cruel and unfair to both my mother and my father. This left my mother painfully alone amid a terrible and enduring tragedy. She had a few allies. My father's psychiatrist, my father's sister, Rhoda, and my best friend's mother, Fern. My aunt Rhoda, as I would experience years later when my father lay dying in a hospital in a coma, was intermittently available. She had a threshold for discomfort and would suddenly take off to Florida and then guilt me for not seeing my father more. I imagine this pattern was the same my mother experienced with her. Lest I disparage my aunt, she truly did her best and was the only family member who could face my father's issues. She adored my father, and he adored her. I adore her deeply. They were allies in the awful home they were raised in. Singing was their passion and escape from their intermittently violent home. Upon seeing each other until my father landed in a nursing home at a young age, they would break into a medley of the standards they had grown up loving. It was always a pleasure to see my dad so happy. So, finally, I am grateful for her. She is still alive at 95 and still pretty clear-minded. My brother and I make the long trip to Long Island to see her when we can.

My dad was actually a really good singer, in the big band style. I imagine singing was always an escape. Our home was constantly filled with music and his singing. I loved it. Frank Sinatra, Bing Crosby, Tony Bennett. Wonderful singers who remind me of my dad. My father was actually compared to Sinatra. He wasn't the singer that Sinatra was, but there was a clear resemblance, blue eyes and all. And when my dad was drafted into the army and chosen to front his army band, I cannot imagine the joy this gave him. My dad loved to be the center of attention. One of the most tragic twists of his life was turning down the offer to tour Europe with the band after his tour ended, complying with his father's wish to return home. It remaind a regret, a painful "what if" for the rest of his life.

Despite the irregularity of his health and his availability, Dad threw his passion, his joy, into being a father. As his firstborn, I was the beneficiary. He was the first baseball coach. At the age of five, I have vivid memories of him throwing me a baseball in front of our summer cottage in Vermont. He showed me how to throw a baseball, making sure my elbow was raised, and I threw overhand. This sparked my life-long love for the game and set me on a path towards my very short stint (due to a serious right shoulder injury) playing for a semi-professional minor league team sponsored by the Atlanta Braves and a few other major league teams.

I have cherished memories of the two of us on Lake Bomoseen next to the same Vermont cottage fishing for hours, row boat afloat; the anchor dropped, night crawlers affixed to our hooks. Years later, the thought of spearing those worms turned me away from fishing forever, but on those lazy summer days (beside the baseball field), there is nowhere else I'd rather be.

My other indelible memory is watching my father, standing on the dock, swim across the lake. I can still see his massively muscular upper body and hear his arms slapping the water with each stroke as he headed across the lake to the other shore. I was a bit scared that a boat would strike him or that he would drown, but as time went on, this was a ritual I looked forward to, his power, his endurance, and his athleticism on full display. It was one of the few times I allowed myself to feel pride that I was his son.

Later, when he was in the myriad hospitals, rehabs, and assisted living facilities, he would see me and let out a yell of joy.

"HOOOOOWARD!!!!" extending the Os longer than seemed possible. That was always deeply bittersweet. His deep expression of love was held in a facility that felt so tragic.

I grew up in a three-story walk-up in Queens, New York, in a neighborhood called Briarwood. It was a middle-class neighborhood in the 1960s and 70s when there was still a true middle class. Its residents were mostly Jewish families and a smattering of Irish, Italian, and Chinese. It was and still is a walking town- schools, shopping, parks, churches, and synagogues all within walking distance from the dwellings, mostly three and six-floor apartment buildings with single and two family homes further away from the center of town. I refer to Queens as urban suburbia. There are not as many trees as in a traditional suburb, not quite a city, but plenty of pavement and brick. These outer borough neighborhoods were borne out of overcrowding in Manhattan and the need for affordable housing. Their construction created an opportunity to remain within the five boroughs of New York City and raise a family. Their design fostered strong communities. Despite the problems at home, I had tons of friends and a terrific social and athletic life. The park with the ballfield and basketball courts was a half-mile walk from my apartment. I spent my childhood moving between school and that park.

I shared a bedroom with my brother Andrew, who is five years my junior. Before he was born, I was desperate for a sibling. Perhaps unconsciously, I wanted another ally in an environment that was already dangerous. When my brother arrived, things went south pretty quickly for me. It had nothing to do with him, per se. It was all the positive attention he was getting. The resources were so slender in our home that to share them with another more needy infant was a huge adjustment. The competition for love continued well into our adult lives, wittingly or unwittingly. This put a huge strain on our relationship, one that has finally abated with only trace residue some fifty years later. Our relationship is yet more collateral damage of my father's mental illness. The shared room wasn't much of an issue. Perhaps there was some shared comfort in proximity. The only time it became a problem was when I sequestered myself in our room doing homework or listening to music and wanted privacy. I was pretty unforgiving in those moments, but what adolescent in any situation is tender and loving all the time? I am pretty sure I was neither most of the time. It was a tough environment, one that a therapist referred to as a war zone years later.

My mom had to endure surgery to be able to have children in the future, and those children (me and my brother) could only be delivered via Caesarian section. She implicitly trusted her gynecologist, Gordon Bemis, a physician at the now-defunct Women's Hospital in upper Manhattan. She adored Dr. Bemis, so much so that she tried to name my brother after him, but I saved him from that fate. One of the things he is grateful to me for is my father's call right after my brother's C-Section delivery (me being the first successful one) to announce the arrival of Gordon Andrew Meyer. When my babysitting grandmother informed me of the name choice, I went ballistic, one of only a few vivid five- year-old memories. Through the din, my father asked his mother what was going on with me. She explained that I despised the name Gordon, I think because of an asshole named Gordon that terrorized me and my friends in the neighborhood. My dad, in a moment of love and clarity that still astounds me, had my grandmother assure me that he would reverse the Gordon and the Andrew. Thus, Andrew Gordon Meyer entered the world.

This was a big deal. It was his turn to name their offspring after one of his deceased relatives- the traditional selection of the first name bearing the first letter of the first name of the deceased person you have chosen to honor. So, by switching the names, he was actually allowing my mother to once again have the naming honor. (The middle name was left to the other parent's honoree). My dad could be selfless like that. And then as petty and vindictive as anyone I have ever known. "The consciousness is vast," one of my wise Buddhist teachers instructed me on the many-sided prism that we all are.

I always wondered why, after all that had been revealed about my father's instability, my mother decided to have another child. She raised that question with me many times in her later years when we would discuss aspects of her life with my father. The answer always eluded her. Logically, it made little sense, but the idea of a two-sibling family was her dream, having been an only child herself. She longed for an ally, a friend within the confines of her own childhood home. And I imagine that the joy of being pregnant with another child on the way helped her forget what her husband was capable of and what the future could hold. It helped her focus on one feeling- love. A welcome respite from the heightening chaos that awaited us all.

Life was hard for all of us, but I have always held that it was particularly challenging for my brother. Not only was the home a dangerous place, but he had a brother who excelled in studies and sports. The shadow, the following-in-footsteps problem. Howard's younger brother. Andrew chose a path, not exclusively, but in the main, of negative attention. Missing classes, underachieving. Even as a youngster, I felt bad for him, surrounded by three very gregarious, big energies. It was not that my brother was a wallflower, but being the low man on the totem pole in age and stature was clearly very difficult. Ill health was always an unlikely oasis for us both; engendering single-hearted care from our mother was not available with any consistency outside of the sick bed. I am sure that is why we both got sick with some regularity. Andrew took this psychosomatic response to another level (unconsciously), developing asthma and later epilepsy. Both of those syndromes abated in his adulthood. Of course, we both had our psychological issues, but those we attempted to mask out of fear for our own fates as much as the fear of our mother's response. She was already underwater with my father, and though she seemed to be on a constant lookout for possible symptoms in us, an actual diagnosis could have tipped her over the edge. And we needed her. Despite her weird and sometimes downright cruel behavior, she was the rock that we all clung to for survival.

****

My best friend growing up was a redhead named David Kornfeld. We grew up right down the block from each other, he on the fourth floor of a six-floor high rise and me on the top floor of a three-story. When we met, we became instant friends and remained so till the day he died from Covid at age fifty-nine. By that time, we were in touch infrequently, and our lives were diverging after we both graduated college. But there was always love there. And always annual check-ins. Until the last four years of his life, which I learned later, had gone very badly for him. His third divorce hurtled him into isolation and depression, which, to anyone who knew him well, was anathema to his makeup. He thrived around people. I wish I could have spoken to him during that time. I wish he had reached out so we could have had one of our periodic New York City catch-up dinners. He was always a proud man, taught that by his demanding father who refereed our little league baseball games (the authority with which he called balls and strikes was always a jolt!), so he was more inclined to tough it out on his own than reach out for help. Not to would have been perilous. Disease feeds on the sad and lonely. David died overweight, with undiagnosed diabetes, alone in a hospital bed during the height of Covid. I attended his online memorial. It felt so insufficient. At one time, he was a respected lawyer, a man with dual degrees in law and finance. Greed and ambition got the better of him, and he made mistakes in his mid-forties that led to his disbarment. I believe he was more a victim than a serious perpetrator, but nonetheless, he got caught holding the proverbial bag, complicit in a deal with a famous client who ultimately took money that had been invested by friends, family, and clients and fled the country for good, escaping legal consequences. After weekend stints at Rikers over the course of a year and public service picking up garbage on the Long Island Expressway, David was never the same. This was my first encounter with a friend who was clearly suffering as much as I was. In his case, he wasn't seeking any psychological help. Their family had always been a "tough it out, rise above" brood. I was in therapy out of extreme necessity but was still unable to face my more profound condition. David's inability eventually killed him.

David and I shared strong similarities- we took our studies very seriously, were competitive in just about everything, and loved to play sports. Our very healthy rivalry in school and on the field of play made us better athletes and students. It never became mean- spirited except for the times we were taunting each other about his Yankees and my Mets. Those loyalties run very deep in our families, and we were the torch-bearers. The fates of our teams prompted merciless taunting and teasing. The Mets owned the late sixties and early to mid-seventies, so I was able to get the better of those years, but still, his defensive retorts were always based on the undeniable dominance of the Yankees over many decades. Or how the Mets choked in the 1973 World Series against Reggie Jackson's Oakland Athletics. But even that never caused any lasting rift. Maybe some hurt feelings from time to time, but nothing mortal.

We were young kids in the middle sixties. Ours wasn't the 'summer of love' sixties. It was the conservative Jewish Queens, New York variety. It was a great place to grow up, but it was definitely a relatively sheltered place. I learned about the tumultuous and fraught sixties in school, in movies, and on television years later and couldn't believe all this was going on outside our secluded neighborhood. The only intrusions were the daily images of the Vietnam War. Those images terrified me. I spent many newscasts under my parents' master bed, fearing that someone from the military would come and conscript me. I lived with that fear until the war concluded. The assassinations, the civil rights oppressions, the antiwar movement, Flower Power, and Woodstock all added tension to the battle raging on in my home, out of view from the rest of the world.

The Sixties was also an era when psychotherapy was being introduced into the culture. It remained taboo for a decade or more, even for the mildest of conditions. Secrets, particularly problems, were held very close lest any family became pariahs. This was the backdrop of my best friendship with David and why most of our hanging out took place at his apartment under the watchful eye of David's very obese but immensely lovable mom, Fern. Though the house often smelled like old meals and the kitchen was always grimy (whenever I see the least bit of grime accumulating on my stove, the memory of Fern's launches me into ferocious cleaning), this became my second home. I used to call her the aorta of the town as she seemed to know everything that was going on with everyone. Her house was an open door and later a place where she looked after many of the working parents' babies and young kids. A burgeoning cottage industry as more and more women were returning to the workplace. The squeeze on the middle class began somewhere in the Seventies, and households were forced to respond. Most of my play dates (I don't think they were called that) back then took place at other friends' homes. It was too dangerous to expose my comrades to the unpredictable behavior of my father. My mother and I never spoke about this; I just understood it from a young age. My playing elsewhere was never discouraged. Who knew what mood my dad would return home in? Since he was a school teacher, he would inevitably walk in during after-school hangouts, thus the evacuation to other, friendly homes.

How early did Fern know about what was going on in my family? I know at a certain point, my very alone mother would finally confide in Fern, but I do not recollect when that began, and I have no idea how discreet she was with our issues. We never got banned from her home or from the community, so if she was short in discretion, she was likely very long in compassion. There were times, as I became old enough to walk down the block on my own that my mother sent me to the Kornfelds when danger in our home was near.

And then there was the incident in the park that announced my dad's condition to the world. Mercifully, that incident never fundamentally altered my core friendships. I always wondered and never asked why my friends remained stuck during that entire event and resumed play as soon as my dad left the park or what they felt or thought about the event. Today, we'd likely hold a therapy session right in the middle of the ballfield, at least in my wishful imagination. Jocks then and now are more concerned with the appearance of strength and health than feelings.

Sadly, I have had no contact with any of my remaining chums since childhood. This has little to do with the state of my family and more to do with the huge transformation I underwent in my twenties, turning from a stable career path that most of my friends chose to the unchartered terrain of the theatre arts. My choice confounded many. I couldn't blame them; it was confounding to me. Once I recognized and accepted that this was what I was meant to be and plunged deeper and deeper into the craft and then the profession, we all became more and more unrelatable to each other.

I encounter many who are intrigued by the process of writing plays or acting, but unless one does it themselves, it is rather impossible to fully understand. In her final months, my mother, who tentatively approached the subject after avoiding it for most of my adult life, revealed how scared she was by how I lived and worked. The letting go, the wildness of the creative terrain.

"How do you relate to me?" she asked in that conversation months before she died.

"We're all different mom. I have come to appreciate our differences," I answered.

A subtle level of estrangement that I had come to accept lifted in that exchange. It was surprising and beautiful.
Though my friends never asked that direct question, my new

operating system exacerbated our progressively drifting relationships. It's no accident to me that I have lost touch with all of those guys. There was a lot of love for sure, but once the years of school and sports dimmed and we began discovering and establishing our adult identities, we never really came to know each other. My mom, sitting at lunch when I was in my late thirties, said to me, "Where did this all come from?" (Meaning my theatre life).

I had no good answer for her. It had been buried for years alongside the rest of the feelings that so deeply and directly inform the artistry.

There was another more pernicious reason I drifted from my friends- my progressively shattering self-esteem. It reached its first nadir in my early twenties and sent me into more and more isolation.

I recently reconnected with an old friend of mine on Facebook, who I hadn't seen in almost forty years. No exaggeration. (One of Facebook's great gifts). I knew him as Modesto, but he now calls himself Sal. When we first connected, he recounted a gesture that had remained with him all these years- when invitations were going out for my Bar-Mitzvah just shy of my thirteenth birthday, my mother wouldn't allow me to invite Modesto, though he was an incredibly close baseball friend who lived around the block from us. I spent a lot of time at his house on Pershing Crescent, learning how to dance in his basement. Some of my first twelve and thirteen-year-old female "encounters" took place in that basement (kissing and petting). I remember learning a dance move called the bump. Does anyone remember that? Not a complicated move, but very salacious for a youngster, which amounted to derrieres bumping into each other on the beat and then some jumps and bumps on the other butt cheek. Exciting! Modesto and I had shared some incredible moments on the baseball field. Me at shortstop, and he at first base. We won two Little League championships together, a very big deal at that age, which yielded tremendous neighborhood cred and attention from the girls. So when it came time for my Bar Mitzvah guest list, Modesto was near the top. My mother nixed his invitation. Why? I have no recollection, but I can speculate that he was the only potential LatinX attendee. It might also have something to do with the goings-on in the basement. I met my first girlfriend there, and I was clearly wooing her with my bumping skills. And then the whole sitting with her during her period thing, which my mother made fun of into her old age. In any event, racism and prudishness aside, he was forbidden to come. Modesto remembers it as him not being Jewish, but that was clearly bullshit because I had a number of white non-Jewish friends who attended. What he reminded me of, which I completely forgot, was that I told my mother that if Modesto couldn't come, I wouldn't be attending either. Radical. Bold. I don't remember ever standing up to her like that during those years when my father was around, providing the potential of frightening disciplinary backup. But… there I am in all the Bar Mitzvah photos, and there Modesto is in all the photos with friends. What a gleaming beam of light that young lad was.

We met on a lovely summer day in the park where we used to play baseball. He asked me to bring my baseball gloves, and I obliged. We had a rousing game of catch, which led to him moving to first base and me assuming my old post at shortstop. It was glorious. All the memories flooded back. He started talking about what an amazing player I was. The best that the neighborhood had seen. Our coach had told me and my mother multiple times that I was the first player he had ever coached (he was in his fifties) who could make the pros. Given all the trauma that we were all experiencing in our home, I remember being flattered and appreciative, but never took that remark all the way to heart. If I had, I am sure he would have been more than willing to become my private coach as I had played for him for three seasons and on a summer traveling team and batted third every year. (Batting third is the "money" position in the batting order).

My baseball career: a casualty of my life living under the shadow of my father's disease.

The choice not to continue playing baseball was made for me as I was accepted into Stuyvesant High School, one of the elite public schools in New York City. (More on my time at Stuyvesant later). Though my parents were proud of my athletic prowess, they were more focused on how elite education could prepare me for a successful life. It was very common among depression-era parents and Jewish ones who knew how easily one could lose everything to make decisions like this. "Letters at the end of your name. They can't take that away from you," one of my successful uncles used to say. So, despite the fact that I had been drafted to play for the new local High School's varsity baseball team as an incoming freshman, I began commuting to the city every day to attend Stuyvesant and gave up baseball. Oddly, I never gave it much thought. This is how it was in my home around the big decisions. My parents made their choice, and I obliged. I could lie, sneak, and manipulate around smaller needs, but not the big ones… until I became an adult.

My favorite teacher at Stuyvesant was Mrs. Grist, my first and best psychology teacher. In those classes, I learned more about the conditions I was avoiding but was still not ready to accept. Of course, she also talked about my dad, which gave me more valuable insight into him. In her class, I also learned about Maslow's Hierarchy of needs. Food, shelter, love, self-esteem, and, at the apex, self-actualization. Despite the formidable obstacles I faced, I determined that day in class to attain what she pointed out was the apex for any human. I was going to become self-actualized. I didn't realize then how deeply I would have to come to know myself and what inner obstacles I had to surmount. But that has always been the principal guiding goal of my life.

During those five years, from high school through junior year of college, I didn't play at all. Just softball games with my friends in the park. Then, a completely unexpected, beautiful, and bazaar thing happened. In the early summer, after I transferred from Brandeis University to NYU in my junior year, I started playing softball games in the south Bronx with my cousin's manufacturing company. I played for the warehouse, where I was working in the business to pay my rent and expenses while I finished college, against the men in the office. The games were surprisingly competitive and brought out my athleticism. I was placed in center field, one of the critical defensive positions on the field. I was still a fast runner and could skillfully track down fly balls. I also had a very strong throwing arm and could sling balls back into the infield with great accuracy.

One day after one of these late afternoon games, my friend who played shortstop told me that the umpire of the games wanted to speak to me. He was the janitor in the factory. We really liked each other. The obstacle was that he spoke no English, and I spoke such little Spanish that we really couldn't conduct a full-throated conversation. Juan, the shortstop, acted as our translator. The umpire/janitor asked if I would be willing to try out for a baseball team that practiced in Central Park three days a week. I had nothing much going on- just school and work, and wasn't in a romantic relationship, so I said, "Sure." That Saturday, I found the team in Central Park, I don't remember where exactly, and began what felt like a very informal tryout. I was out in the field catching fly balls, fielding grounders, hitting pitched balls, and running the bases. The other players were good, and I had a blast. At the very end of the practice, again through translation, I was invited to join the team. What the heck, I thought. "Sure, thank you."

I came back the following Tuesday for our next practice and stood next to the batting cage, waiting for my turn to take batting practice. I was standing next to a very large man, our catcher. He was really welcoming and complimentary about my tryout. I asked him, quite earnestly, what this team was. He looked at me incredulously.

"Do you know who I am?" he said, rather annoyed.

"I'm sorry, I don't."

"Last year, I caught Don Guidry and Dave Righetti."

"I don't root for the Yankees, so I'm sorry that I didn't recognize you."

"It's ok. I was mainly the bullpen catcher, but I did get into a few games."

Then he shows me his World Series ring.

What the fuck? What had I been invited into? He explained that this was a semi-professional team sponsored by a few major league clubs, including the Atlanta Braves—that the league was set up for high school graduates or dropouts in New York who couldn't afford to go to college. Everyone had been "drafted" (invited to play), and it was also a place where former pros could keep playing.

"Why would they want me to play for

them?" "Because you're fucking good, you

moron."

Stunned silence… I hadn't thrown, caught, or hit a baseball in more than five years. And certainly not a 90-mile-an-hour fastball. I had to take in that I really did possess the gift coach Feliciano had said I did. Who does this shit ever happen to? Me. Even in those years when I was just figuring out what God was and if I believed in Him/Her/ They, this felt otherworldly. No effort or intention on my part. It just happened to me.

Storybook ending? Not so fast.

Practicing with the team was sublime. My old form found me much faster than I imagined. Every practice, I felt more and more like I belonged, and the feedback from team mates and coaches was encouraging. Just putting on the uniform was surreal and thrilling. We practiced for about a month until our first game. Much of that time was a blur. My mother was indulging in her new relationship with my stepfather; my father was deeply ensconced in his outpatient regimen in a psychiatric facility in Harrison, NY, and enjoying a new relationship with his co- outpatient girlfriend. I was living in a depressing basement apartment in Rego Park, Queens, and working days and in between practices, going to NYU at night. I was on my own. I didn't tell anyone about the team except a few friends who thought it was the bomb and my dad, who likely couldn't fully appreciate what this opportunity meant. At this point, I had felt so betrayed by my mother and stepfather that I didn't tell them anything at all. After my mother asked my father to leave when I was fifteen, she suddenly depended on me for everything- attention, inappropriate advice about dating, and love. In many ways (until the last ten years of her life), this was the best and most intimate, albeit inappropriate, time in our lives. But… as soon as Joe came into her life, as though all the guilt she had unconsciously felt came raging into her consciousness, she not only cut off all dialogue and connection in the aforementioned ways but started infantilizing me. Her cruelty resurfaced in spades, as though I would somehow pose a risk to her new relationship. Their marriage occurred two days before I left for college. I couldn't get away soon enough.

When I returned from college in Massachusetts to continue at NYU the winter before I joined the team, I was on the verge of a nervous breakdown. Joe, my stepfather, found me psychological support in Cambridge, Mass, and then again in Queens when I returned. That was helpful; they got me through some really rough years, but living with them under the same roof would have been untenable. Instead, I rented that dingy, dark apartment in Rego Park and began working for my cousin to pay the bills. In a bazaar twist of destiny, all of that led me to the baseball magic I was experiencing. Grateful for all that with them. Definitely not. Grateful for the chance to resume my baseball career. Absolutely.

The "What Ifs." If I was in better shape emotionally, I would have had the presence of mind to take a leave of absence from the university and spend every waking moment outside of practice fielding ground balls, fly balls, and hitting in the batting cage. I would have spent the remaining time at the YMCA getting my body in shape, weight training, and running, necessities for any sportsperson and certainly a player playing at the level of my then peers. As is said about what-ifs, "If my grandmother had wheels, she'd be a car." Instead, I hid what I was doing from everyone, my parents especially. My mother and step-father didn't have to say it, but I knew, and they knew, that they were on a constant Howard mental illness watch during those years. Ever since I dropped out of pre-med and began working in and studying business, it didn't help that I was working for my cousin, who they both deemed unstable. I went about my business as if nothing special was happening to avoid attracting too much attention to myself. So so sad. But then again, if my father and mother/stepfather were in a better place when I was showing signs of excellence, they would have hired a coach to work with me privately (like we are doing now with my twelve- year-old daughter. She is a budding soccer star. Chip off the old block?!). During winter vacation, they would have sent me to warm weather climates to play winter ball. Where would I have been by the time I was twenty if all that had been happening from a young age?

Despite all of the training I should have been doing but wasn't, I made the active roster of the team, and though I started on the bench, I was put into the first game in the third inning in right field. In my first at-bat (which would be my last), I hit a ninety-mile-an-hour fastball on the nose but right back to the pitcher. Protecting himself from getting hit, he reacted reflexively and caught the ball, wincing from the ball's impact. I hadn't made it on base, but I was satisfied, and so were the coaches. I had hit the ball squarely and hard. Without the pitcher's fortunate reaction, I would have been standing on first base. That at-bat promised more at-bats in the future and maybe even a starting berth down the line. At the inning's end, I enthusiastically trotted out to right field to play defense with the team, tossing practice throws with our center fielder with pride.

With one out and a runner on first, a ball was hit between first and second base, heading right to me. I moved toward the bounding ball, scooped it up, and seeing the runner on first trying to make it to third, I fired the ball from my position in the right field toward the third baseman, one of the longest throws that can be made from the outfield. As I released the ball, I heard and felt a pop in my right shoulder. In my memory now, it was as loud as a gunshot. I knew at that moment that my playing career was over. This was not a tier of minor league professional ball that paid for doctors, hospitals, and rehabs. We didn't even get paid to play, which is what deemed this semi-professional play. Knowing that I was badly hurt, the manager, coaches, and trainers came out on the field and took a look at my shoulder. I had torn the rotator cuff.

I came back to the dugout and, after the inning, changed out of my uniform, had my arm put in a sling, and bid farewell to the team. It was one of those tough life moments. I knew, everyone knew, that this was the end of the road for me as a player. Praise for my play flowed along with regrets and abundant handshakes (with my left hand!) from all sides. I left the field, never to return to another baseball field. Until that day, six weeks ago in Cunningham Park, Queens, with my dear old little league mate, Modesto, when all of these memories came flooding back.

I came to learn that in a family system like ours, the implicit responsibility of the family is to help the ill member recover or at least keep them stable and happy. This is also true in an alcoholic family system (after my dad left, my mother married an alcoholic). In both cases, the afflicted person's behavior is out of their control. Irresponsible spending, false accusations, paranoia, and major resentments that lead to verbal and even physical rages, are all boilerplate. The belief that anyone can significantly impact another's mental state is proven to be an illusion, But those of us who try, do so out of love and fear. We want our loved ones to feel well and be the person we know that they are when not in the grips of the disease, but we also want to feel safe and get our needs met as children, lovers, spouses, friends, and parents. Imagine a 12-year-old giving his dad a pep talk about self-esteem, reminding him of what a good man he was. Funny, kind, caring... a great athlete. And at other times, reassuring him that his impotency (caused by his medication) would pass. As inappropriate as my role had become, there were times of improvement from this advice, which reinforced my belief that I had some agency over his mental state. Those improvements were always short-lived. My identity was deeply connected to his success, and the perceived failures damaged my self-worth and esteem. As this sense of failure progressed, I lost the desire to be around anyone when I was feeling bad and certainly didn't want to discuss my issues. At that point, I didn't even know what my problems were.

This progressive development of low self-esteem became more acute as I got into my middle teenage years. Rather than attend my local high school and play baseball for a varsity team I was recruited for as an entering freshman, I attended one of the five exclusive New York City public schools, Stuyvesant High School. Stuy was considered the best of the three academic schools (Bronx Science, Brooklyn Tech, the others) in that you needed the highest standardized score to gain admission. This took me to Manhattan every day, an hour and a half commute each way. Being removed from my local Queens routine and status was hard. I was no longer the valedictorian (which I was in my local Junior High) in this elite student body. The city was brand new, somewhat intimidating, albeit exciting. I was no longer at the top of my class and wasn't receiving daily validation. I managed to make the Dean's list every semester, but internally, I was collapsing. And the long journey home from the city every day prevented me from playing ball with my friends who remained at the local high school. It was usually too late, and I had a lot of homework. In addition to all of this, I was separated from my parents during my first year at Stuyvesant. This pile-on sent me into my first prolonged emotional tailspin and revealed my own depression. Losing myself in sports (and the endorphins they produced) and studies (and the attention they brought me) had kept this depression at bay.

****

The annual family escape from the unpredictability and danger in our modest three-story walkup in Queens, New York, was Lake Bomoseen, Vermont, just outside Rutland. My parents discovered this place when I was an infant and returned every summer until my eleventh year. As a city kid, to call it idyllic is an understatement. A lakeside cottage steps away from the lake, wood burning stove for morning frost, frog hunting, fishing (we ate what we caught), a horse that I would feed at the country store, tons of swimming, and a group of kids I would play baseball with on the common field of the cottage community. Sadly, that entire community as it existed then is now a specter from another era. I have visited since, and the entire property has been converted to year-round homes and condos. Gone are the fields. Gone is the charm. At least the memories are real. They remain a vital counterbalance to what was going on in Queens. Far from the grind as a junior high school homeroom, gym, art, and hygiene teacher and surrounded by nature and the lake he loved, my dad would enjoy a psychological reprieve the rest of the year didn't permit. It was there that I felt I got the fullest experience of my dad's true self. It's where he taught me how to pitch, hit, and throw a baseball, swim, and fish. I was able to experience his natural ebullience, a stark contrast to how he would retreat from himself most of the time. I am grateful to have experienced my dad removed from the impact of his illness. During those summers on that lake, we almost resembled a normal family. There wasn't one serious fight between my parents, any irrational outbursts or violence taking place, and no hallucinatory incidents during those summers. Is this some sort of selective memory idealizing that time? I don't think so, but if so, thank God for that. I need those memories, untethered to the darkness we lived through the rest of the year. It must have been amazing to let go, at least partially, from the underlying anxiety in anticipation of my dad's next outburst.

I am told that I took my first baby steps in front of the cottage. In fact, there is evidence of this in a photograph showing my one- year-old self in motion alongside my beaming mother.

There is one memory that belies the relative normalcy of those summers. And it happened at the now-defunct Dog Team Tavern. They are the greatest sticky rolls on the planet. I must have been five or six. We were sitting outside the restaurant, waiting for a table despite having a reservation. Not surprisingly, with 'Dog' in its name, there was a bulldog who roamed outside. He must have been friendly if the owners had given him free rein of the property. But when the dog and I locked eyes, the dog lit out after me. It seemed as if the dog chased me around the entire restaurant three revolutions. The terror of that moment lived on and colored my relationship for years. Today, I love the beasts. In fact, my daughter has a dog at her mom's house who visits here periodically.

Here is the kicker- My mother and father did nothing to stop this dog. Instead, they laughed. They laughed uproariously. And when my mother told this story well into her later years, she laughed still. Even though they probably thought that the dog was playing with me (surely that dog could have caught me and done some damage if it really wanted to), I cannot imagine not sprinting to my daughter's aid if that ever happened to her. After a late-in-life laughing fit brought on by the retelling of this incident, my mother finally apologized for not acting on my behalf. But only after I was able to explain, without rebuke, how scared I was. In retrospect, given the built-up tensions of the year, they probably needed this shared release, but at their terrified child's expense. None of the many other waiting guests came to my aid either. What was wrong with them?

****

The other component of Carl's treatment plan was psychotherapy provided by the same doctor who was prescribing him medicine, Doctor Ed Hanin. As was mentioned, a cocktail of mood stabilizers, antipsychotics, and antidepressants. That name echoed through my childhood. He was the head of psychiatry at the St. Vincent campus in Harrison, NY, and he also practiced at St. Vincent's in Manhattan. My father would have private sessions once a week, and he was uncharacteristically tight- lipped about those sessions, so I never knew what kind of progress the doctor felt he was making. There were many nervous conversations between him and my mother, especially when there was an impending collapse. The signs became very easy to read: hallucinogenic experiences my father was convinced were real, coming home from work at 4 pm and going to sleep for the entire night, outbursts of irrational violence (i.e., the park incident).

Despite the above-mentioned "tells," we were never certain when the full nervous breakdown would occur. This made the home environment completely unpredictable and potentially dangerous. I never knew what I would be walking into at the end of the day. My father was at the mercy of his chemistry, and when the tilt occurred, either during a depressive or manic episode, it was to the Harrison campus of the hospital he went to. Until I turned eight or nine, when my dad was admitted as an inpatient, I was told by my mother that he was going to the "country club." A vacation. I never wondered why the rest of us weren't going with him. Or maybe I already knew.

****

Towards the end of that eleventh summer in Vermont, my grandfather Lou, my father's father, passed away. We packed our bags and abruptly returned home to Queens. We never returned to Vermont again. My dad entered a steady decline that we would never pull out of.

The painful memory that defines this moment occurred at my grandfather's funeral. In the Jewish burial tradition, the closest family is first, and then every mourner in attendance is invited to toss some soil from the dug-up mound onto the casket after it has been lowered into the ground. When it came time for my father's turn, he began violently shoveling, hurling rage-filled expletives and blame along with the soil. My father was incredibly strong, and it took five or six men to remove my father from the gravesite.

My grandfather Lou was an incredibly complicated man. I only knew him as he was succumbing to arteriosclerosis, which is now associated with Alzheimer's disease- stoic, affable at times, but basically non-communicative. They say that in his prime and beyond, he was a virile, gregarious man, but legend tells of a younger man and father who would fly into emotionally and physically violent rages against all of his children. My dad received the brunt of his fury. Male competition, jealousy, who knows? His sisters received their share, but never as frequently as my poor dad.

Lou was also, by all accounts, mentally ill. A man, like my dad, whose beast was frightening. I am sure that despite the terror, my grandfather's displays somehow gave my dad permission to give way to his own doppelganger. Many times, when my father's darkness was released, throwing a bottle of juice across the room or putting his fist through the wall, he would cry with regret. I mean, down on his knees, sobs. As if during the violence, he was possessed and, in the aftermath, realized it was actually him. I have no idea whether my grandfather's mental illness was responsible for his rage and violence, but it is hard to imagine that it wasn't, at least in part. And I never heard one story about his monstrous tirades ending in weeping, at least, by him. They say he might have been bipolar as well, or perhaps a severe depressive, though there was never a diagnosis. My oldest cousin reports having deep, loving moments with him. I love and trust my cousin. He was the first-born grandson and probably got the best of Lou in the same way I came first and got the best of my dad. I came on the scene later and never experienced any of Lou's kindness and generosity. My father's sister, my aunt Rhoda, remembers a father who didn't like my father in his younger years. He behaved ragefully at worst and disinterested at best. This must have taken quite a toll on my young father, who was perpetually attempting to garner approval from my grandfather, which was never forthcoming. Quite a contrast to my cousin's memories. Mental illness has been well-established as a chemical and behavioral illness. Trauma enhances the symptoms and severity of the episodes. My father and I had plenty of work to do on the traumas we both faced.

****

The first time I visited him in the mental institution, I was twelve. I am sure I pushed and pushed, and my mother, in the midst of all the confusion and with a dearth of babysitting options, simply brought me with her. I wonder if she ever asked Doctor Hanin if that was wise. Patients who are in a facility like this are, at best, temporarily unable to function in society and, at worst, long-term patients with chronic mental health challenges. My father started as the former and, as his life progressed, became part of the latter. I witnessed the full measure of this population while posturing as the together, mature, and caring son. It was anything but together on the inside. I was terrified. Random screams coming from inside rooms, attendants rushing to the scene, men and women roaming the halls, usually with assistance, some making overt passes at me, near comatose patients sitting at tables being goaded by well-meaning counselors to engage in art. The entire place was permeated with this smell, kind of like turning milk combined with chemical cleaners. I have never smelled it again except on subsequent visits to the same mental hospital, which, sadly, I had multiple opportunities to replicate. How many times was he admitted? I

39

would estimate ten or fifteen extended stays until he became a perpetual outpatient throughout his fifties. I have visited many hospitals both as a visitor and for minor surgeries (hernia, appendectomy, and tonsillectomy). Thank God, never for mental illness, and they never smelled quite like that. I could never eat in the guest cafeteria, where we could take my dad for a meal. Though the food looked palatable enough, the idea of eating in there made me gag.

In my freshman year of college, I was called by Doctor Hanin. My father had fallen into a catatonic state (not his first), and even the electroshock therapy that he had recently been subject to was not helping. Electroshock therapy was one of the most traumatic indignities my father experienced. After enough of these treatments, something essential changed in him. Gone were the irrational rages, but those treatments also removed parts of his personality: his exuberance, his pluck, his passion, his strenuous, sometimes funny, and often wise opinions, and his high energy. He never lost the joy that he retained when not in the middle of an episode but was forced to trade the depressions that necessitated these procedures for a substantial loss of his vitality and charisma. That was very hard to see.

Since the electroshock wasn't breaking the catatonia, they thought if I could come to visit him, it might help. What was I supposed to do? I was drowning in my own immaturity and ineptitude at college in my freshman year, but I agreed to come. This role of trying to fix my father was very familiar. The next day, in the middle of my travel preparations, the doctor called to say that he had come out of it after they told him that I was on my way. The problem was now solved; I didn't have to come.

In actuality, that deep connection my dad and I had, the one that filled him with love and anticipation, was also a tremendous burden of responsibility, leading me into places and situations no young person should be exposed to. Events like this also perpetuated and magnified my savior complex. Though my father was in some ways soothed by my presence, this was a far cry from delivering any kind of lasting salvation. That sense of responsibility for my dad's mental health was an albatross that prevented me, in many ways, from dealing with my own maladies. In fact, it bolstered my sense of will and emboldened me to do more, be better, and keep the focus on him and off myself until I couldn't anymore. I had been in therapy since I was eighteen, but at the age of twenty-eight, when his girlfriend left him, and he succumbed to progressing Parkinson's disease, it all became too much for me, and I crashed.

I had become an astute, ready reader of people and expressions, taking the temperature of a room in nanoseconds. But when it came to taking care of myself, I was probably ten emotionally. Arrested.

****

My most important therapist, Carol, and a childhood summer camp friend turned therapist, urged me to try Alanon. This was initially confusing since the Alanon Program is designed for family and friends of alcoholics. They told me that the family dynamic orbiting my father's mental illness was practically identical. I went. I spent the first few meetings in the back, crying. I completely identified with nearly everything I was hearing, which kept me coming back. Soon, Alanon was part of my weekly healing regimen, attending meetings all over Manhattan. In fact, the people provided such support and comfort in those meetings that it became the safest place for me to be. For the entire second year, I attended at least two meetings a day. It was as if the deep block of ice that my emotional life was encased in was slowly and steadily being melted by the love and support of my fellow attendees. I mentioned discovering fear on travels earlier; Alanon revealed the vast depth of my fear, as deep as a submerged iceberg, which most days felt too much to handle. In that safe environment, I could feel all of it and then take it into therapy to work on the causes of that fear.

Why Alanon and all twelve-step programs work is very hard to explain. The steps are irreplaceable and provide a very clear path. Central to all of the steps and the philosophy of the twelve-step world is a belief and appeal to a Higher Power of each person's understanding, which, in my opinion, is its genius because many people come into the Program with a nonexistent or fractured relationship with the concept of God. There are also the slogans which are simple anchors to return to during the day. My first long-term sponsor, when I said to him, "These slogans are from nursery school," replied, "Welcome to nursery school." And he was right. Keep it Simple, Easy Does It, One Day at a Time— these ideas were so basic, yet so foreign to me, as I had never learned them in my disease-plagued home. I think the greatest factor of the healing is the fellowship, the people. We are all applying all the above-mentioned tools, without which there would be no program, but the support and love, the nods of acknowledgment when one is speaking, the hugs and thanks for my shares at the end of meetings, invitations to be the lead speaker at a meeting. Also, witnessing from week to week how my fellows were processing their pain. That gave the rest of us encouragement to process our own.

For those first two years, on some level, despite all of that, I still felt like a fraud. Though no one in authority (there isn't an authority in the program, which is part of the beauty of it; we all are equals) checked my credentials, the explicit statement in the Traditions is that this is a program for those who have been affected by someone else's drinking. I shared this with my sponsor (an elder who helps the "novitiate" through their paces), but he didn't make a big deal of it.

"If you identify, you belong."

But on some level, I still felt like an imposter, like I was stealing something that shouldn't belong to me.

Then the inexplicable happened. My stepfather admitted he was a lifelong alcoholic. His and my mother's marital issues had put the relationship at risk, and one day in their couple's therapy, he fessed up. Can you imagine living as an alcoholic, closeted even from yourself, from the age of twelve when he took his first drink to almost seventy? And he functioned incredibly high, which previously supported his belief that he didn't have a problem. But this, his second near divorce, shook him out of his denial.

It was a eureka moment - I could now get my Alanon Union card stamped! The beauty of all of this is that my stepfather Joe's admission introduced him to AA, which he had been devoted to for the rest of his life. He never had another drink again. It also moved my mother into Alanon and for an extended period of time, my brother as well. We were now a family in recovery.

It was explained to me that those who were in the program were also addicts, afflicted by an addiction just as powerful as the one that alcoholics suffered from. They refer to AA as the wet disease and Alanon as the dry one. The alcoholic is addicted to the drink, and those in Alanon are addicted to fixing and "helping" the drinker or anyone with a serious, tragic problem. As mentioned earlier, I refined that addiction living with my father. I had to let go of that compulsion to fix. All the tools of the program provided us with new tools and taught us new, healthy habits. We were all encouraged to build a relationship with the God of our understanding who we could abdicate our loved one's care to.

Alanon introduced me to a healthy relationship with God or Higher Power. The phrasing was key: the God of my understanding. I had no understanding, so I was really starting from scratch. It was more than non-understanding. As mentioned earlier, it was fear due to my dad's devotion. From the moment I became conscious of his devout belief, the idea, the concept of God, was associated with his mental illness.

My then-therapist illustrated something that I have never forgotten. She compared my life experience and understanding to a file cabinet filled with files on all life subjects. My "God file" was empty, except for my dad's relationship to God. It was time to find my own relationship.

The suggestion from Alanon was to "Act As if" I believed in a Higher Power and begin "turning things over" to Him/Her. At first, it was small things, like a worry or a low-risk decision I had to make. After finding relief and aid from these experiences, I began turning over weightier concerns and bigger decisions. This is how I built my relationship with the "God of my understanding," which I still refer to as the God of my non-understanding. To me, God is more of a consciousness, a force of care, if I choose to solicit that care. I knew where my self-will had gotten me. I came to know that I needed the guidance of this force and that guidance has proven consistent and unflappable. If it weren't for that relationship and this program, I don't think I would ever have been willing to seek the medicine that altered my life. Care. The acceptance of healthy help in the forms that it appeared. That care and guidance were sorely lacking in a reliable way from any authority figure I had known.

I walked into Alanon suicidal, hopeless, and doubting my entire direction in life. I remember sitting in private therapy sessions at the Center for Core Energetics on East 23rd Street with my therapist Carol (who I worked with for eighteen years!), who recommended I come to Alanon months before I started attending meetings and hearing loud sounds coming from down the hall.

"What is all that noise?" I asked.

"A group therapy session," she explained.

"Oh, that's not for me!"

How had I gotten to a place where being around people and sharing our common problems was so aversive?

Living in a home where mental illness was the norm and thus the taboo that accompanied it, my inner life got very tribal. I was part of my clandestine family circle of dysfunction, which demanded my loyalty, my only confidante, afflicted with the same low self- esteem, paranoia, and non-existent trust as I. And those confidantes were not confidantes at all - no one could really talk about what was actually going on inside them. We could fret about the day-to-day exigencies of our tenuous existence, protect each other from assault, and visit our loved ones in the mental hospital, but talking about what was going on inside of us was too risky. And furthermore I don't think anyone really even knew what was going on inside them. Fear, certainly, sadness, maybe, but none of us were in touch with the more far-reaching behavioral and emotional side effects. During our early years, my brother and I were too young to really comprehend what we were in the middle of. We were constantly living in crisis, sort of like a war zone. Denial, repression, and hiding, became a way of life.

As mentioned, I had a huge and tight-knit group of friends growing up, and I loved and cherished those connections. I had entered the theatre world where collaboration is at the root of creation, but somewhere along the line, I had become nervous and insecure around people. Before I entered the program, I was ashamed of my perceived stagnation in life. In my mind, I was a failure. Sitting in any room with a bunch of other people in pain was completely anathema to me and completely contradictory to the image I had developed in my early years: the leader, self-sufficient, a success with glowing prospects. I was ashamed to have fallen this far.

One early December morning at the age of thirty, at the very bottom of the bottom, I staggered into my first Alanon meeting. A few months earlier, I had woken up on the lawn of my then-girlfriend Lena's parents' property after a crack-of-dawn fishing excursion followed by a long sleep. Right in front of us was her father's work studio, a monument to this man's huge success. Something broke inside of me that morning. I was turning thirty. What did I have to show for my existence? What of the high expectations from the former valedictorian? In my mind, nothing- a foray into theatre and acting studio ownership which ended in embers, working for my cousin again at the job I despised, teaching a small acting class in Teaneck, New Jersey, and my father's health on a steep decline. I needed to fall this far in my own mind to finally recognize I needed more help. Once and even twice a week, therapy wasn't enough any longer.

The relief I felt was almost immediate, what they call the Alanon Pink Cloud. My sponsor had instructed me to -

"Sleep, eat, work, go to meetings, make calls. Keep things very simple." I followed his advice. On some level, it was all I was capable of for the first two years.

I made friends—recovery friends. Not day-to-day running mate friends, but folks who I could trust, count on, and relate to. They formed a collective of unconditional support and love.

Thus began the long and painful journey of recovery. As is said, recovering myself. This was still years before I received my official diagnoses and medication, but the alchemy in those rooms remains a necessary piece of the triage- Therapy, Alanon, and Medication. The trifecta widened the margins of my self-understanding and provided the essential tools for my healing.

One vital differentiation I learned was that isolation was very different from aloneness. An extreme episode of low self esteem, like an acute episode of depression, would send me into isolation. Low self-esteem is the precursor for comparison and shame, always feeling less accomplished, less capable, and less everything. Depression has always been shameful, evoking the same comparisons and also, as expressed, complete disinterest and alienation.

I am a writer, which requires aloneness. When I am in a good space, I relish my time with myself. Writing is not just two or three hours sitting in front of a screen or a pad; it's also time for reflection, daydreaming, napping, and wandering around. Letting the subconscious do its work. In this place, going to movies, traveling, hiking, and playing golf by myself are all delightful. No pressure to make conversation. Just being and doing. And once I have had my fill of that, I am nourished and eager to return to the world of people. Isolation is sitting in the darkness; aloneness is refreshment. Aloneness requires feeling good about myself and at peace with what I have done and who I am. I can't say that feelings of isolation are a thing of the past, but I feel like isolating hardly at all, and when I do, I know it is a sign that things are going astray, and I have the tools to get out of that place.

****

It is not unfair to claim that I was raised by two diseased humans. My mother was afflicted by narcissism and possibly a degree of borderline personality disorder. My mother's mother was by far the singularly most narcissistic woman that I have ever known. My grandma Fanny, or Fran as she liked to be called in her post-death-of-her-husband phase, would have made the worst narcissists wither in her presence. Not an easy start for my mother.

She, like my dad, was not without her many merits. She was super strong, fiercely loyal, deeply loving, incredibly smart, and had a rapier wit and sense of humor. She enjoyed dishing it out and appreciated the skill in others. She hated being the butt of jokes. The necessity for my now forty-plus years in therapy was caused as much by her behavior as my father's. Again, to be fair, she was surmounting formidable odds, not just with the toxicity of my grandmother but marrying my dad with his wealth of problems. As they say, the deck was stacked way against her.

She and I had many, many fights, even before my father, her

48

disciplinary enforcer, left the house when I was fifteen. Even before ten years old, I had a threshold for her abuse. During many of these altercations (which usually were just verbal, but my mother was not shy about hitting me when she felt backed into the corner), she would move to the closet in my bedroom and point to the top shelf where the suitcases were stored:

"If you don't like it here, pack your bag and leave!" It's terrifying for a seven or eight-year-old. Where was I supposed to go?

Mom's struggles brought out the worst of her: toxic fear, intense control, and a loose tongue. The Quotables are extensive. Here are a few:

In the wake of getting my first C in my life (this at college in organic chemistry, the death blow to my and her dream of me entering medical school):

"Stop sticking your dick into all those women and start focusing on your studies." (As a freshman in college, not only was I ill-equipped to take care of myself as a human, but it was near impossible to get any women to take a serious look my way.)

When I was preparing for my first of many outpatient procedures to restore my esophageal passage to normal size (more on this soon), and my then girlfriend wished to attend:

"Either she comes to the hospital, or I do."

All of this invective was venom-laced, with an idiosyncratic left eyebrow moving vertically for emphasis, her signature tell of imbalance, irrationality, and rage. The message is that I would be kicked out if I didn't fly right. This attitude and control style permeated all of her interactions with my brother and me when she felt the least bit threatened or scared, which I imagine she felt a lot living in that environment.

These regrettable episodes and her irrational accusations and subsequent escalations with both of us led my brother, a veteran therapist, to conclude that my mother suffered from some functional mental illness herself. He speculates either extreme narcissistic disorder or possibly borderline personality. This would explain the mean, rage-filled outbursts that punctuated our childhood and led my father to his defensive violence. If you knew that a man, much larger than you, could be led into retaliatory rages that led to dangerous violence exacted upon you, wouldn't you work on strategies of de-escalation? My mother was in therapy. And she was incredibly smart. The only conclusion that we could arrive at is that she had no control over her own need to be right. That somehow being wrong posed a mortal threat to her. Into her old age, she was capable of those same irrational rages; I just got better at avoiding her triggers. For years, I would step into her crosshairs. Years of therapy and Alanon helped me alter my responses to her insulting comments. Mercifully, her incendiary comments became less and less frequent over the years after she had entered Alanon. In the program, it is said that "the family situation is bound to improve" by following Alanon's ideals. It did. I learned how to be less reactive and then nonreactive, recognizing and finally accepting that this is the way she was. One of the Alanon questions is "Do you want to be right or happy?"

When I was thirteen, I developed a stutter. Not a pronounced one, but enough to tie me up when I was trying to defend myself, and especially when I was met with aggression. This happened most always at the receiving end of my mother's verbal assaults, challenging me for any action of mine that pushed her the least bit off center. Something as innocuous as not cleaning my room to getting a grade less than an "A" on any exam. It's hard to fathom today, as I speak (and write) for a living, sitting in front of actors as a teacher and director, audiences before shows, and also in front of rooms (and sometimes auditoriums). The stuttering thing rarely enters my mind. The process of writing this brought it back into my consciousness for the first time in many years. I am so fluent, so confident. When asked to speak, I immediately agreed. The slight stutter comes up on occasion but surfaces these days as a stammer or feeling slightly tongue-tied. A hint of its former very oppressive self. I pay tribute to my recovery.

But back in those days, the stutter in those situations was crippling. Sometimes, during sleep, I dream of being verbally challenged by someone and not being able to get any words out. My awake self can physically feel my inability to speak. It feels, in those moments, like an actual disability, my intense, often angry emotions wanting to burst forth and my mouth, my voice, unable to express itself. In contrast, in life, no one can get me to shut up! Amazing how the fear embedded in childhood, in a real, daily, life-and-death struggle (my therapist referred to my youth as a war zone), can remain in the unconscious all these years.

Flash forward to the early 2000s. I am fifty (I came to parenting late in the game, thank God, when I was in a reasonable state of emotional health). My mother, despite her best efforts, predictably, had strong opinions about my daughter's behavior because, well, she had strong opinions about everything. In fact she was the authority even on subjects that were remotely known to her. Speaking about Lena's famous father:

"He can't be famous. I've never heard of him."

Thankfully, by then, I had acquired fairly good skills at either rolling with her volley of judgments or using my twenty-plus years of Alanon and years of therapy to redirect her. But there were times with my daughter when my fluidity was put to the test, particularly with recurring themes that my mom just couldn't let go of. My daughter's eating habits bothered her and sometimes enraged her – picking at food, not finishing her plate, not liking French fries (a travesty!), and eating our food, and not her own. I tried to explain that every expert I had read said that complaints and hyper vigilance about eating do not lead kids to compliance and can even lead to eating issues. (Case studies one and two, my brother and I rose with those same eating judgments). After telling her this multiple times, she finally agreed to stop, but her compulsiveness would engulf her, and after a meal or two, the complaints would begin again.

My daughter could get oppositional around my mother. We were driving out to see her like we often did, and with all sincerity, my then seven-year-old asked,

"Was grandma nicer to you when you were a

kid?" Two years earlier, at 5, my kiddo asked,

"Why does grandma always have to be right?"

There was this one emblematic occurrence during this time. My daughter and I were having an issue. Her excessively cranky attitude was stressing me out because I knew that my mother took it personally and always wanted a "happy visit." I was attempting an attitude correction, and my mother intervened, which stressed me out even more. In a fairly even-handed way, I asked my mom to allow me to handle it. She persisted, so I pushed back harder. I led my mother out of the room.

"I have a wealth of experience that could help," she insisted. "I'm upset with her mom. Let me handle this," I replied.

"What about my feelings? I am upset, too." Her lifelong refrain.

When my mother is upset, no one else's feelings matter more than hers—not even a seven-year-old's, especially not her granddaughter's father, who happened to be her son. She knew I had just told my wife earlier that week that after a year and a half of separation, I wanted a divorce. None of that mattered at that moment because my mom was upset.

Quickly, things ratcheted up to toxic levels. Rather than honoring my mother's feelings (I had just driven three hours and had the week of wife talks that led to the divorce decision), I got angry. Huge mistake. In the last fifteen years of her life, I was pretty good at avoiding this anger no-fly zone. My mother's upset and my anger was a toxic combination. But I was already angry at my daughter and was primed for a reaction. The rest was predictable. My anger led to my mom's heightened control and outrage, which ripped off my scar of being treated this way by her as a child, and we were in Gonesville.

A man should never ever hit a woman (I never have), and that was on my dad for allowing himself, or his disease allowing him, to go there. But my mother, knowing my father's penchant for resorting to his hands and knowing he was an unstable character, would back my father into an intellectual and emotional corner, rendering him completely impotent and unable to defend himself verbally. Though my dad was street smart and quite wise, she was his intellectual superior, and not by small measure. So when she backed him into that corner, delivering her verbal kill blows (win at all cost), he would do the only thing he instinctively could do to survive her: punch his way out. Shut her up with his brawn, which was formidable. To be fair, when I get going, I have been told more than once that my anger is scary, and with my mom's PTSD from my father, I am sure her fear was at a fever pitch. But to say that right in front of my daughter felt like the deepest possible betrayal of trust and the cruelest thing anyone has ever said to me. I had already committed the crime of making my mother feel wrong, unheard, and silenced in relation to my daughter, and laced with anger, she probably experienced her own wounds, deeply stabbed, and she retaliated. But to utter those words as a mother to a son?

"Call your psychiatrist. You are out of control."

The only person I ever heard my mother say that too was my bipolar and schizophrenic father. Not only had the scab been ripped off my primal wound, but a knife had been stuck deep into it. To utter those words was to categorize me with my father: a mentally ill abuser.

To essentially call me crazy and, later in the evening, "sick," and then tell me:

"You need help. This happens all the time; your daughter told me so," right in front of her, it was beyond the pale.

This was the sort of cruelty my mother would resort to when she felt hurt or threatened. Anything to neutralize her perceived aggressor. I tried to de-escalate, but after long periods of silence and attempts at détente, she would return to how I mistreated her, and when I attempted to defend myself, she demanded that I take my daughter and leave.

"I am eighty-one years old, and I cannot take being treated like this. Get out. Get out!!"

But whether eighty-one or forty-one, she had zero ability to self-reflect and could never concede any wrongdoing, whether she was unhinged or calm. In her mind, she was never wrong. In our sixty-one years together, she only apologized one time to me. One. And that was because of the mandate carried out by the Alanon ninth step. The amends step. She had entered the program when my sixty-nine-year-old stepfather finally revealed his lifelong alcoholism. To save their marriage, they both agreed to go to their respective programs. The only thing she could muster in that amends was how she was critical of me growing up. Complete amnesia or inner defense of the rest.

So, with Chanukah gifts (this was the first night of Chanukah) and wet laundry in tow, my daughter and I hastily packed our bags and left. I had to uncomfortably return twice to retrieve things I had inadvertently left. The second time, she yelled:

"Will you take all your stuff already!!!"

My mere presence was too much for her. Some five years previous, in a fight likely similar to this one, my brother got tossed out into an equally cold night. He was from San Francisco and, with no car, was forced to take a train into Manhattan from Long Island and connect with another to stay with my in-laws in Westchester. This is what she was capable of: a complete and utter emotional shutdown. Her beloved, caring sons were temporarily disowned.

I'm not totally sure how we came back from that one, but we did. It took my brother three years, one year of silence, two of letter writing, to finally talk to her and another year to risk being in the same room with her again. I was subject to her one-sided prosecution of my brother; she was only comfortable seeing him when she deemed him "changed." My brother learned the rules.

Internalized them. Stay away from the no-fly zone. Enter it and be exiled.

The miracle, which I can only attribute to Alanon, therapy, and acquired wisdom, was that for the last fifteen years of her life, with few exceptions—the above episode being one of them—we entered a phase of love and care. As long as I didn't cross into the danger zone, things were okay.

When she passed away fairly quickly from the effects of pancreatic cancer, we had become great friends and very close, perhaps for the first extended period of our lives. I had taken her to many doctors' appointments and looked after her in those final months. I am very grateful for having been in the right heart and mind to do that. We shared some of our most intimate, honest moments in those final months, like her finally questioning me about my career and the creative process I recounted earlier.

****

I was depressed long before I knew what that word meant, long before I sat in front of a psychiatrist. Despite an iron-clad posture of denial, I was finally diagnosed with Major Depressive Disorder at the age of forty-five. This is a very serious condition characterized by month-long bouts with severe debilitating depression. I was broken enough to finally accept my first 'script' from the doctor, who is partially responsible for saving and then restoring my life. Even the word 'partially' betrays my lifelong belief that somehow I could fix myself or be fixed with the right depth of psychotherapy, primal scream, Buddhist retreats, years of Alanon, the right amount of courage, the right amount of vulnerability. Feel deeply enough into the pain buried in my childhood, and all would be well. It was when I was forty-five years old when my then-wife said, "You have an anxiety problem," on our way to yet another of our Buddhist retreats in Cooperstown, New York (as a former semi-pro baseball player and longtime fan, the irony of that still doesn't escape me), ensconced in the pit of maybe my fifth or sixth downward spiral of our then ten-year relationship, looking for another meditative fix.

"This time, this time, I'll commit to even more serious practice," I would say each time I went to a Buddhist retreat, often in one of these depressive phases.

My ex's "you have an anxiety problem" comment was so simple, so well observed, so obvious. Still, it was hard to accept at that time- anxiety was the symptom that pointed most directly to the root.

Some of the initial signs of my depression, not that I was anywhere near admitting there was an issue at that time appeared during junior high school in the park, in between pick-up basketball games. I was thirteen. I would be on the sideline waiting my turn to play and a heavy, numb feeling would descend. I would become listless, not sure if I could pick myself off the park bench, let alone compete on the court (somehow, I would muster up the energy). Where did it come from? Why? It felt deadening. This was such a stark contrast to the aliveness I felt on the ballfield, the place that would so effectively mask or move the pent-up anger, rage, and fear. They say that endorphins are an antidote to depression, but on those days, I could never get it going. Like I was a few steps slower, moving through something thick, dense. There were days I was even disinterested. Easy to see from this perspective what a red flag that was.

I was on an elite traveling baseball team in my last year of junior high, age fourteen, and had been recruited to play on the varsity team as an incoming freshman at the local high school, but my sports skills were beginning to flag. Though I was still hitting a hearty .425, it was the first time in my young career I was afraid of having the ball hit me, and at a shortstop, that is the kiss of death. So, even if I had become a Hillcrest Lion the following year, who knows how long I would have lasted on the team?

From the age of fifteen to seventeen, I traveled on the express E or F lines with all the "suits" transferred at Fourteenth Street and hopped on the L cross town to First Avenue. An hour and a half on a good day, door to door from my Briarwood, Queens apartment to the front steps of Stuyvesant High School. The commute replaced my mid-week after-school sports. Gone were the daily boost of endorphins. Though my parents were incredibly proud of my athletic prowess, the brain path took precedence. My mother, throughout her life, bragged that I could have been a pro baseball player (which turned out to be true in the unlikely fashion explained above), but she couldn't support all the choices (including not going to Stuyvesant) that becoming a pro entailed. I was recruited as an incoming freshman at Hillcrest High School, but my parents never gave that a moment of consideration or gave me the choice. Jews of that generation valued degrees. MD, PhD, JD. Letters at the end of your name. Jewish immigrants who came to America with nothing believed that those letters could never be taken away.

So, the acquisition of them became prized, encouraged, and supported, emotionally and financially.

I endured so many days on the train, falling into the dull sleep of depression, almost missing my train stop a number of times, and then waking up to my life. Every time I awoke in those states, I wished that I was still sleeping. Being awake in that depressive feeling was almost too much to bear.

That was the last summer my folks were together. It was in the air almost every day. Violence. Screaming fights in the middle of the night. And still vivid in my mind, and the last straw for my mom, was when my crazed dad, made crazy by some innocuous remark, cornered my ten-year-old brother in our tiny third-floor kitchen and raised a clenched fist. My dad had bruises on his arms for days from the pressure of the grip I applied to allow my brother enough time to slip out. I was reminded later that my brother, in his underwear, ran terrified out of the apartment, down the three flights out the building's front door. He was discovered sometime later, hiding behind a bush. This was the backdrop of my entry into Stuyvesant High School.

****

There are two major types of depression: Major Depressive Disorder (MDD) (also referred to as Clinical Depression) and Persistent Depressive Disorder (PDD). MDD can last for several months and is usually recurrent. PDD usually lasts for two years. Gratefully, in this context, I suffered from MDD. I cannot imagine how untreated folks with PDD can bear it, knowing that when they enter this phase of depression, they are looking at the possibility of a two-year term. My terms of three to five months seemed endless and unendurable until the meds kicked in and became fully effective. Two years filled with that? I wonder what the rate of suicide is among folks with that level of severity. They say that PDD depression is less intense than MDD but carries the same symptoms. Two years is a very long time for any degree of depression.

Yesterday, I gave money to a homeless fellow who has been standing all spring on an entrance ramp from Route 9 south to the Mid-Hudson Bridge in Poughkeepsie. This is the third consecutive spring I have seen him standing there with a cardboard sign that says, "Out of work. Need a job." I wonder if anyone has ever stopped to offer him employment. I do the only thing I can do. I offer him my spare change as the traffic backs up, and I can slow it down and pass it to his appreciative hands. My daughter reminds me when we see him, "Give him money, Dad." "God Bless You," he always says. I noticed that this year, he is walking limp. Does he go to a shelter during the cold weather months? I am always in awe of how he and folks like him have the humility to stand out in the street day after day and ask for money. Some say these folks are scamming the rest of us, that this is actually their form of work. Most believe they are using the money for alcohol and drugs. But I have a soft spot in my heart for some of them. There is something about the urgency with which he rushes to the car when I slow down and open the window that moves me. "There, by the grace of God go I," I think almost every time I slow down. When I go to Manhattan, I reserve one dollar for each trip to give to someone on the street in need. How do I choose? I don't know. I just know the person when I see him/her. Sadly, there are always a variety of people to select from on each trip. When my daughter accompanies me to the city, she looks forward to the moment when we give that person the dollar. If the person doesn't look dangerous, I let her drop the buck in their makeshift receptacle.

This is a tradition I hope she continues long after I am too old to bend over and deposit the dollar.

I founded an Acting Program in the early 1990's. I co-teach with my dear friend and the godmother of my daughter, Rachel. Whenever a student who seems a bit different or socially challenged enters her class (she teaches the beginners), I am called in to meet with them. Many of these folks are on the Autism spectrum, and most have a degree of Asbergers. I seem to know how to relate to them. I speak to them like I would speak to anyone. I am not sure how they have been treated in the past, but I make them as welcome as I can, teaching them where they are. Many of these students thrive in our program. Often, they move from our beginner level into my advanced class with me, leap- frogging over Rachel's intermediate level. As compassionate as she is, Rachel feels that I am better equipped to deal with them on a weekly basis. It's my depression, I am certain, that makes me more sensitive to these folks. I also lived around my dad my entire young life. Despite the constant danger lurking, I always had a sensitivity and empathy for him. The beauty is competing with the darkness. I know that given the right or wrong set of circumstances, that could be me standing on the street corner with that sign or entering an acting class with severe social anxiety. When a disorder makes you feel that debilitated, that dependent, imagining that makes some kind of sense. I played a homeless man on stage. In fact, I played two different homeless men in two different plays. To prepare for the first role, I spent a night in the streets in the West Village in Manhattan, a very nice part of town. A gushy enough assignment as neighborhoods go, but I spent the entire night terrified. I encountered homeless territoriality and late-night gay bar patrons trying to buy me sex. The second homeless character was schizophrenic. I had familial research to draw on for that one. I brought myself fully to both of those roles, possibly the best performances of my short-lived acting career. How many among us could survive on the streets? Many of these folks get pushed out of mental institutions. Some make it into shelters. Some do not. I once read an article about a man who lived under the streets of the city in an abandoned tunnel for years. He would emerge to panhandle and buy food and then disappear. We are adaptable creatures. My fears of that fate have waned over the years, but they still lurk, even in times of great prosperity. When I was in my twenties and well into my forties, this fear controlled me. Unconsciously mostly. Every time I felt the least bit depressed and scared, I would throw myself deeper into sports, deeper into studies, deeper into music. Even after the depression took over my life during the commutes to high school after my parents came apart, I attempted to push forward. Despite that, I pushed on until I collapsed in my freshman year of college in Massachusetts. Eighteen. What that young man didn't know at the time as that he would need to remain in therapy for another forty years to sort out and make peace with his traumatic childhood. The irony, explained later, is that it took me til my mid-forties to finally accept the medication I would need to help control my problem. All the therapy was necessary, and without it, I would still be in deep trouble psychologically, but receiving medicine meant admitting that I was like my father. A notion I wanted no part of at the time.

My brother, a psychotherapist in San Francisco who has dealt with his own depression, also possesses this empathy. He has built an entire community in the Java Beach area comprised largely of disenfranchised men. Some are formerly homeless - a few who still are - most former drug or alcohol abusers, and all are living on the fringe. I have met many of his friends. All have big hearts. All love my brother, and he loves them. Perhaps this isn't the community one aspires to when growing up, but it's the one my brother has chosen as his crew. They are beautiful people who have witnessed and experienced the cruelty life has to offer and have survived. Same as my brother and I. Growing up as we did, we share a similar perspective to folks like them. Mental illness is always lurking. We were exposed to a completely contrary perspective to the vast majority of the world.

****

My dad's body was stocky, muscular, overweight and also soft and smooth, especially around his shoulders. That smoothness always got my attention when he would embrace me with his incredible hugs. The smoothness always caught me by surprise. Something about his roughness and his potential brutality. There is something about hugs that I find essential. In those moments, there was no illness, no trouble, just closeness and a feeling of pure love. I have never felt as loved as when I was enveloped in one of his epic embraces. And he always smelled great. His natural smell. Why, I am sure natural smells unfettered by perfume or cologne remain so important to me.

But there were boundaries that were crossed. Many moments of inappropriate use of force that would become too intense, playful hits to my arm that would too often be too hard. And then his unexpected violence.

The shower door opens. I am naked and wet, water streaming down from the shower head. My father's fist flies into the stall and delivers a blow to my upper thigh. My brother's arm gets broken in the aforementioned brotherly play on that snowy

Sunday watching football, and Carl finds me feeling guilty and terrible, and he delivers another blow to my leg. And, of course, the cross-the-ballfield strike and humiliation. What made all those moments even more shocking was that until I hit puberty, my father would never hit me. I mean, never. I was his golden boy. He would do anything within his power for me. Extend great kindnesses, keep little secrets from my mother, make me laugh, and champion my every accomplishment. How did I square all of that with what followed? Not easily. To this day, I am wary of excessive kindness. It takes me a long time, years in some cases, to fully trust. When will it shapeshift into violence and cruelty? I experienced the same confusion with my mother. Generous, funny, smart… and the next day, the next hour, a torrent of hostility. At the time, I felt privileged to be taken into his confidence. Advanced. Mature. Special. I had come to see that when I began resembling an adult post-puberty, his actions, and words had little to do with me. They were all generated by this inner desperation to express his pain, whether it be with his fists, his aggressions, or his words. I would come to understand this later, first hand, when I began experiencing my emotional difficulties. Suffering is self-involved. There is so much focus on the feelings and the problems that any attentive listener provides a valuable opportunity to offload.

There were the very, very intense wrestling matches we would engage in on my parents' bed. Once that happened, my mother would come in and stop us because she was sure that he would inadvertently hurt me. But now I wonder if she was also aware of his sexual confusion, and she, even unconsciously, sensed that the body-to-body contact was just a bit more satisfying to him than she was comfortable with. I never asked her about that. That would have potentially opened up an entirely new can of guilt and shame she already felt remaining married to him for so long.

Sadly, there was damage that was far worse and longer lasting than the eventual blows I did endure. My father's sexual dysfunction and confusion weighed heavily on my pubescent self. Here, I was emerging as a sexual being, and those concerns and issues were swirling around in my head. Before long, I was obsessing about these issues. I was undeniably attracted to girls, but to test that theory, I started inserting homosexual fantasies into my mind. Those fantasies never evoked attraction or arousal, but the fear that I might be incited continual testing in my mind. By the time I hit fifteen, this untethered stream of thoughts had finally led me into despair. I finally discussed them with my stepfather, Joe, and then my mother's boyfriend, who was a psychiatrist. Despite his own alcohol problems and his inability to disagree with her, he cared a lot for me. Those talks were incredibly helpful, and finally, the relentless perseverating lifted. In those days, Joe was an enigma. I really, really liked him. And what from this vantage point was clearly inappropriate or at least an overstep, he would ask me for advice about my mother, which I gave freely… because I liked him and wanted it to work out. I thought for sure I would have a new healthy ally. I mean, he was a psychiatrist. But there was also something with Joe that didn't add up. As gregarious as he could be, he also had long stretches of silence where he wouldn't talk at all. What I would learn later was that my dear stepfather was a career alcoholic.

****

There is one other fateful moment that lives inside of me permanently. I can still see it clearly. The packed suitcase was on the floor, my father and myself, and my mother was standing at a safe distance from him in the tiny vestibule in front of the kitchen. Carl was in a winter coat and hat. I was standing there at the age of fifteen to protect my mother in the event that my father lost control. It's this tableau that is branded in me. The last moment of our family. I was filled and am equally filled now with a complex of feelings- relief that he was leaving, that there would be no more threat of physical violence, a deep sense of unmooring (who would we, I, be after this moment?), afraid, poised for violence, and deep sadness. Despite it all, all the abusive, inappropriate behavior, I deeply loved my parents. And this was it. He would never set foot in that three-story walk-up apartment ever again. And there was a palpable sadness between my parents. What I am sure they knew, or at least my mother knew (we spoke about this many times since) - if it weren't for the horrible disease that continued to plague my dad, that moment would never have happened. Beneath all the awful behavior that their situation elicited, they were good, caring people who loved each other a lot. That is why they fought to stay together for twenty years. The tragedy of that might have been the hardest to accept.

In my memory, we stood there a long time, though it was likely just a minute or so. And then, my father picked up his suitcase and proceeded down the hallway into the dining area and out the front door. Deep quiet. Then, my mother's tears. I know my father never forgave my mother for this decision.

Given my father's worsening condition, this was the only possible outcome. If the situation had continued, one of us might not be here as my father's violence was escalating. My brother remembers (I don't) Carl threatening my mother:

"If you leave me, I am going to come back and kill you all."

Was this an idle threat, a power play? A moment of delirious sadness? We do know that this has happened. Too regularly, I hear about this on the news with disbelief. How could a once-loving family devolve into slaughter? Andrew also told me that for months after my father left, he slept with a bat under his bed. Mercifully, my father never acted on this threat. I think deep down, I knew he wouldn't. My dad loved me and my brother too much, and the threat must have been born out of deep despair - How would he go on living without the support of the family? He did, but he was never the same person after that.

I wasn't the same person either. The necessity for my parents to split was undeniable, but from that day forth, I have had a mistrust in the sanctity of family. The most fundamental foundation for any child's life, even a fifteen-year-old child, is their family. If I couldn't depend on that, what could I depend on? It cast a long shadow not only on my desire to have a family but also on people's trustworthiness.

"Mom, are you and Dad going to get a divorce?"

This was the refrain from either my brother or me the day after every one of their monumental fights.

"No, honey. People who love each other fight. It's perfectly natural. Your father and I are not getting a divorce."

Trusting any companion in any relationship- friendships, business colleagues, and certainly intimate ones- is still a challenge. It takes me years to settle into a relaxation with the person. Fortunately, I have had many positive and long-standing relationships to help heal this wound. But for the first year or more, I am always "looking for the lie." Can the person be trusted? Will they hurt me, leave me?

****

Is it any surprise I would need older male mentors? They were all loving and very skilled in their particular ways, but all were deeply flawed in familiar ways. Leo, my first twenty-five-year-old mentor when I was a teenager, reported sexual conquests, including those at the now-defunct sex club Plato's Retreat. The elderly producer-director who wanted to perform fellatio on me in my twenties. The first important acting teacher who would clandestinely neck with the female student, I fancied. The master acting teacher, who I learned was receiving blow jobs from certain "privileged" girls in his office during class breaks. The soon-to-be-famous actor who attempted to go too far with every attractive boy he met, including me. But despite all of their flaws and excesses, each man revealed and supported important parts of myself. They helped reconstruct me, rebuilding one layer at a time. They reassured, and validated my talent, my uniqueness, my individuality. They all brought timely and necessary gifts. Even the ones that wanted something in return. Somehow, I was able to hold my ground in every instance. I never gave in to the unreasonable, not once. Compared to what I had received from my sick dad, this felt easier to manage. It probably wasn't, but I felt like a pro, uniquely qualified to rebuff bizarre male adult behavior. The positive gifts offered were necessary and far outweighed the cost.

Right as my father was leaving when I was fifteen, Leo, the twenty-five-year-old Plato's Retreater, entered my life. A legend in the neighborhood park, he was terrific at every sport and eventually took me under his wing. He also lived right across the

68

street from me, and I was invited up to his apartment many times. It's where I perfected the art of preparing omelets, which I prepared for us both. It was a way I extended gratitude for his attention. The timing of this attention felt perfect with no father around. Leo's age clearly concerned my mom. She never said as much but was clearly worried about potential untoward behavior. She protested at times but never intervened. She didn't have the bandwidth as a newly minted and freaked-out single mother and, on some level, was probably glad that someone had taken an interest.

He invited me to play in adult basketball games, and I was asked to join his highly competitive adult YMCA touch football team. I was the only teenager on those squads, but that didn't surprise anyone. I was tall for my age, and fast, and had hands like fly paper. If you threw the ball anywhere near me, I would catch it. It evoked envy from my friends and boosted my confidence. There was an aspect of our relationship that, at the moment, felt "super cool" and a privilege. Like my dad before him, he would share graphic details of his sexual escapades with his girlfriend and his many visits to Plato's Retreat, where clearly anything went. There were illusions about a recent ex whose memory weighed on him, but that seemed, to a pubescent teenager, unimportant compared to the pleasure of conquest and delights he reported as an unattached single man. These stories, combined with his pushing me to lose my virginity, catapulted me into a rigid campaign to do just that. "Jump in the game."

At that time, and as I imagine most oversexed teens our age did, my friends tossed around lies like a salad. Nothing I recall that ever involved intercourse, just bragging about a lot of touching, kissing, and the occasional blow job that rarely, if ever, happened. But there was something about that final frontier that hung like an albatross around all of our pubescent IDs. I was at Stuyvesant High School as a fifteen-year-old and was bound and determined to bring back the chalice of first intercourse to my mentor. Most girls wouldn't look at a first-year student (an experience I would re-enjoy as a freshman at Brandeis University), and hardly any of them would be the help-a-young-dude-lose-his-virginity types.

There was this one girl, sassy and smart, whose reputation, correct or not, preceded her. She seemed to take a liking to me, particularly when I lied about having sexual prowess. The fallacy of this was quickly revealed when somehow I got her back to my apartment in Queens from Manhattan, an apartment that I was expressively forbidden from bringing any girl back to, particularly with sexuality of any kind on the brain. There was a window, a short window, to pull this off. My dad was now living elsewhere after my parents' recent separation, and my now-employed mom was due home from work in maybe an hour. I have no idea where my brother was, but he wasn't there. I proceeded in my childhood bed to prematurely ejaculate before accomplishing the deed. And despite generous or possibly felonious offers from her of "let's try it again some other time," I was determined to succeed. Luckily, it doesn't take newly hormonal boys any time at all to reload. And the next time, we consummated. But, to say that it was one of the singularly most unpleasurable, loveless moments of my sexual life would not be hyperbole. After the relief and thrill of having accomplished my goal quickly wore off, the disgust and disappointment from the underwhelming, even shameful, experience arrived and stuck around for quite a while.

Then there was my second encounter. That summer, I met a young woman who I quite liked and even began to love. She was the horseback instructor at the day camp where I was a counselor. She taught me how to ride horses, and I hoped I would afford the same tutelage in bed. But here is the rub: I lied about my age. She was a nineteen-year-old soon-to-be sophomore at college. I wasn't quite sixteen. The roguery of the lie never sat well with me. She was so nice and just a good all-around person. Karmic repayment for the deception awaited me at the end of the summer. She wanted us to wait to consummate (another example of her maturity), which we did, despite many a night of petting and happy ejaculations for us both. But on that late summer night, days before she was leaving for college, we left for Jones Beach. We had spent many mornings in her bed at her home, so I am not sure why the act had to happen in a clandestine location. Probably had something to do with the gravity of the act if caught. I am not sure who selected the dunes at Jones Beach, but at the time, it seemed like a very romantic setting. Moonlight, the sound of surf. And it was all that until the night patrol moving up and down the beach in their four-by-four started shining flood lights in the direction of the dunes. Understandably, but not to that almost sixteen-year-old, I lost my erection. Could it have possibly been because it felt more like the scene of an amphibious beach invasion than lovemaking? Did my guilty conscience lying about my age all summer factor in? She was so compassionate and understanding, completely grasping the impossibility of the moment. I was horrified. This was the second botched intercourse attempt in less than a year and equally as awkward and unpleasurable, not to mention totally unsexy. And, of course, there was the matter of owning up to my age lie. Dishonesty has always plagued me, so much so that telling the truth, however painful, became requisite for any measure of pleasure or peace in any area of my life.

Before she left for college, I just couldn't pluck up the nerve to come clean. We didn't try having intercourse again but parted in each other's favor with promises to remain in touch, which we did. On her first return home, which I am pretty sure was her Thanksgiving break, we went out and had a wonderful time. Dinner, laughs, shared sweet memories. All was well and good until we pulled into a secluded part of the Long Island Railroad parking lot and started to neck. Sex began, and intercourse happened, but once again, I came prematurely. My inexperienced terror of being caught in a running steamed-up car, the lie still hanging over me like a guillotine. After we finished, I was disgusted. I revealed the lie in, I am sure, a less-than-sensitive way and summarily broke up with her on the spot. She was in shock. I fled the car, never to be seen or heard from again. In Alanon, we have a step (eight of the twelve) that encourages us to make amends to all the people we have harmed. I have never been able to track her down. She is one of the very few to whom have not been able to make amends. I feel bad about that to this day. The best I could do was commit to never treating another woman like that again. And since I hit the rooms of Alanon at the age of thirty, I don't feel like I have. There have been women who have been disappointed by me, but even in those disappointments, I think that I have acted with dignity and respect for their feelings.

Compassion. For all the women I hurt and for the terrified boy who was confused about his sexuality, running as fast as he could away from his sick dad. Who desperately didn't want to become the mentally ill father he loved, who, at the age of fifteen, wanted to please his more than slightly inappropriate mentor. Who wanted to live up to the nickname of "Machine" he had acquired on the field of play.

It was thanks to a few very terrific and experienced girlfriends in college that I finally got sorted out sexually… mostly. I did have fun, satisfying coitus in an actual bed (and never again in my mother's home) within the confines of my first long-term sexual relationships.

****

I started dating a woman in 2018, Hannah that, I thought, was the next big thing. We met in Woodstock right after my separation, and my daughter and I moved from my family home to a temporary apartment in New Paltz. Hannah is beautiful, smart, spiritual, deep, intelligent, and sexy- all the attributes I have been drawn to my entire life. The circumstances of our meeting were entirely different from the 'swipe right' variety I became voraciously engaged in. She is a friend of a parent at my daughter's school who actually introduced us… in person. Shortly thereafter, we became "friends" on Facebook. We began exchanging periodic "how are you doing" messages, likes on each other's photographs, and greetings on birthdays. We even bumped into each other at the occasional school event where she was considering enrolling her daughter. It was always really nice to see her, and we appeared to have a mutual attraction. As sure as I may be about a woman being attracted to me, I am usually as wrong as many times as I am right.

After my legal separation became official, my Facebook status changed to "single," and our messages became more frequent, and their tone became increasingly intimate. At this point, she was in the middle of a contentious divorce, so understandably, she was not ready for dating. Six months later, she announced that she was divorced. I plucked up the courage and asked to "see" her. It was lovely. The chemistry seemed abundantly present, and shortly thereafter, she confirmed her attraction. Our first kiss was electric, which opened the door to many more make-out sessions (yes, folks in their fifties and early sixties still make out). Heavy foreplay soon commenced but always stopped short of intercourse. I have found that adults near my age tend to proceed with a certain degree of caution sexually when they sense a potential significant connection. Impetuousness and impatience of youth give way to awareness of longer-term implications after crossing the sexual Rubicon. There did seem to be a certain kismet to the proceedings. I was sleeping over at her place for the first time, and after we had engaged in a long session of petting short of orgasm, we decided to just snuggle and sleep. Just before I nodded off, I noticed a strong luminescence coming through her window right behind the headboard. I rose and saw that it was coming from over the horizon. My mind immediately ran through options: aircraft of some kind, a light show, an alien ship. Moments later, it became clear that a full orange moon was emerging just over the horizon. I nudged her. We both stared out the window, watching as it rose further. We both turned to each other and knew without speaking that we needed to make love, which we did under the moonlit canopy. It was the most intimate love-making experience I had engaged in since the best years with my ex.

****

There comes a time with whomever I date, if there is a potential for staying power, when "the conversation" has to happen. My major depressive disorder. Depression has a certain conventionality to it nowadays. There are a gazillion books on the shelves about depression. They seemed to move from the self-help bookstores to prominence at Barnes and Noble somewhere in the early 2000s, I think, as Oprah introduced it so fluently into the American Cultural scene. But Major Depressive

Disorder. The word *disorder* is what tends to trip people up for a good reason. The anti-fantasy went something like this - a wonderful woman, right for me in so many ways and me for her, but this condition is too great a risk for her to live with. And when she hears about my father's Bipolar disorder. Forget it. The last thing I see is feathers floating in front of me, like the road runner in the cartoon leaving Wile-E-Coyote in his/her dust.

My dad's first fiancée (the woman he was dating before my mother) broke off their engagement. I imagine it had something to do with his condition. When he met my mom, he chose not to mention anything for fear, I am certain, of their relationship meeting the same fate as his previous one. I have been reminded constantly over the years that I am not my father and that our conditions are extremely different. The fear of rejection still exists. What woman would want to commit to a man with a mental illness? Most people have no idea what the condition actually is, and for those who are not up on all these things, it would be easy to imagine the worst. I do not have the same ailment as my father, but… when I get into an episode, it was and still isn't easy for me or the woman I am with, whether we're cohabiting or not. I can fall into a deep and long depression. (Much more on this later) In my life, outside of intimate sexual relationships, I keep this information very close. As far as we have come with the recognition of mental illness and really good medical support for those who suffer, we can still be met with subtle or not-so-subtle aversion and fear. Thus, it is important, professionally, to keep this to myself. However, with intimate relationships, there has to be authenticity and transparency, which means letting the person know exactly what I, and in turn, they, are dealing with. This is a specter that has accompanied me throughout my post-separation dating life since my diagnosis was rendered mid-marriage when I was forty-five.

With Hannah, I was a little less worried because, well, she is also a therapist and would likely bring compassion and understanding to my condition. When the day finally came, she brought all of that, but she was also concerned. Her long-term ex also had a mental illness, borderline personality disorder, which can be almost impossible to live with and equally hard to treat. The person can be pleasant and kind for a week or more, and then when their system gets triggered by fear or pain, they turn judgmental, angry, and mean. It was understandable that my condition would give her pause. She knew that I took my mental health very seriously and that the medicine was working. The upshot was that she needed time to digest and process. I completely understood that. Then Covid hit.

****

There is another mental obsession (a defense mechanism I learned later) that arrived on the cusp of any serious romantic commitment. Let's call this persona the Problem Accumulator: inventorying faults about the object of my affection.

"Her voice is too high pitched."

"She's cute but not gorgeous." (Even if she is actually

gorgeous). "She could stand to lose 10 pounds."

These mental fixations appeared when I met my most important girlfriend, Lena, in my late twenties and again in my late thirties when I met the woman who would become my wife. Gratefully, the items on the list paled in comparison to the many positives possessed by both women. And who can get in the way of a deep soul connection? The same list began coalescing around Hannah, this lovely, soulful woman. But here again, the list of positives was undeniable.

****

The last word on my mentors and sexual boundaries. My primary Buddhist teacher throughout my thirties was eventually exiled by the communities who supported him and introduced him to the United States (he's British). I saw him on multiple occasions, in his very charming fashion, flirting with young, attractive female yogis. But as we all learned later, he ended up in bed with a number of them. Brilliant, a serious dharma transmitter, a laser- sharp speaker unparalleled in my experience, who could deliver a searing talk extemporaneously. This was a man that I went to sit in meditation with in India because of his brilliance. And he was brilliant there as well. Powerful. Helpful. But as he had said, "the consciousness is vast." Later, when he was found out, he made excuses about not returning to the States because he wanted to decrease his "carbon footprint," but we all knew what footprint he was being prevented from increasing. Here, another of my flawed mentors. Or maybe human is a better way of stating this. But I don't know. When one is preaching human aspiration, it is surely disappointing when a basic tenet is transgressed. Many have fallen victim to the same transgression. Men in power and their feckless abuses have been brought into the necessary light during our so-called "Me-Too era." There is a deeper level of the Inferno that belongs to teachers, religious figures, mentors, therapists, and guides. Particularly those who are dealing deeply with the delicate areas of students' psyches and wounded histories. I take this predatory behavior very personally. There are occasions where a teacher legitimately falls in love with a student and the student with the teacher, and after careful consideration and ample time, something more serious is embarked upon. The time recommended by the therapeutic professionals is three years. Longer, shorter? Who is to say precisely that every situation is different? I have known teachers who end up with former students and have long-lasting, happy relationships and marriages. But that sort of consent and serious consideration is very different than acting upon momentary teaching intimacies. The student often projects their needs, fantasizes, and pedestalizes the adored teacher. There is something villainous about a teacher preying on students' longings and moving the relationship into the bed chamber. Or at least narcissistic. And yet, and yet, and yet…. That man helped me. And I miss him. And I am sure many other people do as well. How do you square with that? "The consciousness is vast." This mentor's indiscretions provided a great lesson in what not to do. But this is another example of a mentor with leaky sexual boundaries. Four or five of them possessed this same defect. No surprise, given the sexual confusion I came from, that these were the kind of folks I gravitated to.

****

At around the age of twelve, food began to get stuck in my esophagus, right at the opening to the stomach. I told my mom what was going on, and she blamed the problem of eating too fast, which, to this day, I am sure I still do. I wanted to get away from the table. Fights would break out between my mom and dad at dinner fairly regularly. I would leave the table under the guise of going to the bathroom and make myself throw up to dislodge the piece that was stuck. As time went on, this problem recurred with such frequency that I became incredibly good at dislodging. So good that I became able to induce vomiting without sticking fingers into the back of my throat. Despite my best efforts to slow down while eating, the severity of the instances increased until one day, when I was eighteen and a freshman in college, I couldn't get the food out. I was taken by a friend to the emergency room, where the piece of food was removed for me. I was put through a battery of tests, and it was discovered that I had a condition of progressive narrowing of my esophagus. This narrowing was caused by a buildup of cartilage forming a ring right at the base of the esophagus, near the entrance to the stomach. They urged my mother and stepfather to take me to see a specialist.

The specialist, a stern man whom I experienced more as a marine sergeant than a doctor and who was the head of the gastroenterology at my stepfather's hospital, prescribed a muscle relaxer. He also urged my parents to get me in to see a psychotherapist as quickly as possible. This gruff man, despite there being very few case studies on this condition, knew something deeper was up. After all, I had been through, it still amazes me that it took this medical condition for my parents to finally get me into therapy.

My brother and I desperately needed therapy years before, given the trauma we were experiencing on a regular basis. My mother was concerned and asked my father's doctor about therapy for us. She was told to keep an eye on how we were functioning. And we both were, in our early years, doing well enough that she accepted this instruction as fact. Given that advice and the era we grew up in (in the 1970s, therapy was still being assimilated into the culture) and the constant challenges she was dealing with at home, her misreading of our situation is understandable, I suppose. Perhaps if she had been willing to face my eating condition sooner, that it was not only my rushing at the dinner table that caused these episodes, but more dominantly about what was going on with me emotionally, she would have sought help at an earlier age. Perhaps, perhaps, perhaps.

And then there were the dilatations. In the first three years after the condition was diagnosed, there were ten procedures — you read that right, ten—to tear the cartilage around the esophagus and restore the eating passage to a normal diameter. Today, that end can be achieved with one or two procedures as the entire process has become automated with a gradual enlarging of a thick balloon inserted with a scope down the food tube. Back then, I had to help by swallowing a metal coil that would gradually enlarge to the desired diameter and be snaked down my throat by the doctor. There were so many procedures because the doctor feared rupturing the esophagus by pushing down a coil with too large a diameter.

As I understand it today, this psychosomatic condition was a rebellion by my body not to ingest any more of what was going on around me. And taken to its extreme, a desire not to exist in that reality any longer. Unconscious suicide. This all came out slowly and painfully over the course of many years of therapy.

There was another young sign that should have been more evident, and it is hard to believe it was overlooked or more likely rationalized away, though it's hard to understand how.

When I was ten, I started banging my head on the floor of my room when I couldn't sleep. No one in the household thought that was odd. Sometimes, I used a pillow to deaden the sound. Other times, my head made direct contact with the linoleum. No one ever came in to see what I was doing. Shockingly, it never woke my brother in our shared bedroom. Like some kind of integrated white noise (he, to this day, uses white noise to sleep). My mother definitely heard it. I know this for a fact because she would apologize to our elderly downstairs neighbor about the sound. She would tell her that something had dropped during the night. She should have apologized for the jack hammer construction work taking place at night over her head. The lovely old neighbor never seemed to question it. I do remember that it made me feel better. Did I ever concuss myself? Somehow, that act of repeated banging did something for me. What? Quiet the noise? Distract from the negative self-messages that were beginning to gather in my head? Did it help with my depression, my adolescent version of electro-shock? I also spent a fair amount of time rocking at the bottom of the bed. (I just went to the bottom of my adult bed to check. Definitely soothing. I think I'll pass on the head-banging re-enactment even though there are no longer any downstairs neighbors.) Did my mother tell Dr. Hanin about this? I never asked her.

I would like to report that after ample therapy, those strictures magically disappeared. They did not, though the time lapse between dilatations has increased dramatically. I haven't had one in five years; the one before that is longer. Everyone has places on their body where stress and tension gather. This is mine. And gratefully, it is being managed. I do need to be checked once the food starts "sticking." Food gets down there, and it takes a few moments, and often, some liquid is needed to help move it down. I also have acid reflux (another manifestation of anxiety), and an increase in the dose of the prescription antacid often does the trick. At those times, I was also checked for signs of esophageal cancer, which is still a killer. All the ripping and tearing in this area has put me at higher risk.

****

I can go into any crowded café and write. I am doing so right now, in the Harvey Milk terminal at San Francisco International Airport on the way to visit my brother. I have always been able to concentrate in crowds. I can block out all the chaos around me and laser focus. For a long while, I couldn't sit in silence. I needed music when I studied or did homework. Too much unresolved internal weather and too many times external arguments I just had no room for. The music quieted the external and internal noise, and somehow, I was able to concentrate. I could sit at my table in our shared bedroom, turn on the music, and hyper-focus on whatever homework assignment was in front of me. And I got A-s. That was never the goal. It was a reflection of this heightened escape. It became a safe place, one where I could feel smart, productive, and normal. One day in the ninth grade, I was approached by the assistant principal. He informed me that I was a few percentage points ahead of a young lady for the distinction of valedictorian.

At that moment, becoming the valedictorian turned into a competition. I knew how to compete on the field of play in practically any sport. I had talent as an athlete and that arena provided me a necessary retreat and escape. The homework table provided the same solace. And in pursuit of becoming the valedictorian, that table became another field of play. Come the end of the scholastic year and graduation I was named valedictorian.

On the field of play no one had first names. Nicknames, last names: Meyer, Oscar (as in Oscar Meyer), Machine. Or the number you were wearing on the back of your jersey which, for me, was always 3. "Hey 3." I got used to all of that. I liked it. Being identified by a moniker or a number. Perhaps it allowed me to slip into another part of myself more easily. My first name wasn't used much or at all. Howie, maybe. Sometimes, but Howie didn't do justice to my level of achievement on the field. Machine. Meyer. 3. More fitting. It was a high to get locked in to those zones of play- that level of performance and the respect that it engendered. I get why career professional athletes have such a near-impossible transition out of that high. I came crashing off of that in my brief stint in Low A ball. To feed on that every day, combined with that unique performance camaraderie, was intoxicating and addictive. There was something intensely intimate in that athletic camaraderie. One hears that from war veterans. A deep love for their platoon mates, all pulling together towards the same end, looking out for each other. On and off the field of play, you never had to utter a word about your feelings or what was going on at home. Maybe feelings about a girlfriend or potential girlfriend, but that would always trend toward the lurid. I never liked that.

There was a perfect safety in that domain: channel the anger, hit the ball, run fast, and win. The math was simple and easy to follow—in my case, easier than most to execute. That was my best childhood therapy. Thank God for it.

There was another incentive for success in both arenas. I grew up in a home where good news was in famine-esque supply. These distinctions were a balm for the entire family. A place for all of us to be reassured that maybe there was something redemptive in all this after all, to feel that we weren't as doomed to the loop of suffering as we actually really were. And I am sure quite unintentionally, the more I succeeded, the more attention I received and the more love I felt. This unleashed an inner force that would haunt me as the years progressed. The validation beast. And then the pressure to remain a success. And who can do that every day, every year? But I sure tried. Until I couldn't try anymore. That early creeping then galloping depression saw to that. But for a time, it was sustaining and a counterbalance to all the lurking disease.

The first C in college began to capsize the belief that I was a Superman. My folks, my mother, in particular, were devastated. What had become of their valedictorian, their future world-beater? I had been semi-effectively keeping the feelings of failure at bay, and now I had theirs to bear. Ah, the inescapable nature of the praise-blame dyad. That was the chief precipitator of the fast decline that characterized my first year in college. There is no way one can attach one's worth to what the world thinks of you. The topography is too treacherous. The fall is too steep. So how can you be in the world without any attachment to that? First, I would have to begin to understand why I was so sad, so afraid, so angry, and, at times, so listless. The esophageal diagnosis and subsequent remedy began when life in therapy began. I say "life" because from the time I started therapy at age eighteen, I virtually haven't stopped. I no longer go weekly (I went twice a week in the days where I needed triage). Tough to confess? Yes. Smart? Yes. I joke that I could own a small island with all the money I have spent on therapy in my lifetime. Those healers are among the most consequential people I have had the privilege of meeting and working with in my entire life. Can you put a price tag on that? And what would I do with an island without all the therapy. Be miserable and alone and then dead. And have some good swims before I off myself.

My earliest memories of the joy that came from my parental

praise and feverish expectations of scholastic success started from second grade, when after a year plagued by garden-variety illness and copious sick absences, I was demoted from the high level first grade class (super intelligent or highly achieving) to a far lower level class (dumb as far as my parents were concerned). After a parent-teacher conference that brought further concern to my parents, (I hated the teacher which probably accounted for a portion of my less than lackluster results), it was made more than abundantly clear that "you are much, much better than this," "you'd better start performing, or else," etc. Immediately, I was not allowed to watch TV before all my homework was finished. As educators, my parents took my education very seriously. But my performance carried even higher stakes. I will never forget coming home from one of those parent-teacher conferences, the teacher reported more of my underperformance, and my mother's fingers attached to my ear, pulling me up the long banister leading to the back entrance of our apartment building.

"I will never sit through a session like that again, you hear me? You better shape up or ship out!!" Once again, the prospect of being kicked out of my home. I had only one option, I thought-Perform. And perform I did. Until that C in my freshman year of college.

Maybe even more motivating than being kicked out or the withholding of love attached to success was the thought that if I could perform at a high level, then maybe my mother would be convinced that I didn't possess the malady that my father had. When I did resume performing at an extremely high level in second grade and was reinstated in the top tier class in third, never to be demoted again; it brought extreme relief to my mother, which in turn brought a measure of relief to me. In her fear and inexperience she would be on constant mental health watch with both me and my brother and told us as much. Somehow prowess on the sports field brought a similar brand of relief. How could a highly functioning student and star athlete be afflicted by mental illness? My mom talked about both late into her life. "His Little League coach, (probably one of the first alcoholic mentors), told me he is the first kid I have coached who could have made the bigs (the major leagues)." This was a big deal coming from him. For all of his beer-slugging, he was a terrific coach who had done it for a long time, taught me a lot, and was very effusive about my abilities straight to my face.

The coup de grâce. In the same year, I was named valedictorian of my junior high. I was scouted and invited by the local high school to join their varsity baseball team. My mother long and cruelly joked, "That was the year he peaked."

That valedictory moment was formative. It was a much-needed boost of confidence, which was also highly addictive. There were proud smiles slathered across my family's faces when I rose to make my valedictory address at the graduation ceremony, and the standing ovation from the entirety of my racially integrated class. Receiving that ovation, which the black and brown students initiated, was even more significant. We never shared a class together, but we had formed that athletic bond I explained after three years competing on the field of sport. I'm not sure why, but their applause felt more genuine.

I liked the spotlight, the adulation. "He can be anything he wants to be," my ninth grade English teacher told my mom.

But at that graduation ceremony there was something on my father's face that I had never seen before or had been too frightened to notice: jealousy. He and my mother had just separated, and he was heading into the psychological slide his life would never recover from. But there it was. I had surpassed him and he didn't like it. Every action has an equal and opposite reaction. This was mine. The success he had been so proud of through my adolescence reminded him he had done something good, something important in his life had mutated into my betrayal of him. After that moment, our lives would irrevocably begin to diverge. Though for a period in my late teens and twenties, I tried like hell, unwittingly, to accompany him on his downward slide, the rapidly waning bond that we shared was mainly nostalgic at that point. Yet it felt too vital to let go of. But even through that time, and perhaps the saving grace of that time, my addiction to being deemed "great," "special," and "a star" kept propelling me onward.

The peak of "greatness" is a lofty one and I have never reached that apex in my baseball and theatre career to my own satisfaction. The force that was born very early and fed on that stage in junior high school threatened to destroy me in my adulthood. Any number of depressive episodes have been catalyzed by the expectation of being deemed great by the industry with all the associated opportunities. I have attempted to explain that in many different ways over the years—wanting it too much, trying too hard, introducing my acting, directing, and writing to people of influence before my craft was at its peak, bad fricken luck. God is readying me for greatness. Hah. The one I have settled on, half-jokingly, as a studied spiritualist, is that in my past, I was a very recognized and arrogant asshole. Any accident that I have encountered plenty in my line of work. They are completely self-centered humans and many narcissists. Is it a coincidence that as I have become more humble and less full of myself, the celebrities who are also more balanced have appeared? I don't believe in coincidences anymore. On one level, it's what these professional pursuits engender, and the handlers encourage and enable. The PR is all about them all the time. Is it any wonder that these folks go through relationships like soiled underwear? Poetic and ironic: the moments I am able to lay down that hunger, that longing, is when my greatest career satisfactions and successes have occurred. No lurching has ever brought that about.

It took me three quarters of my life to learn that and was a plague that affected all those around me. It certainly contributed to the ending of the two primary relationships of my life. Thank goodness it began to wane when my daughter was born. I am pretty certain that her arrival was the primary driver in putting it to rest for good.

But, however deleterious that motivator would become, striving for greatness scholastically and the adrenalin and endorphins produced during sport kept me afloat during those early years. No wonder my mother was convinced that all was well and that I didn't need therapy. More. That I was special. Chasing that distinction, despite the casualties it produced, did enable significant achievement. Even if one falls short of GOAT's (greatest of all time) status, much can be achieved along the way. Starting a professional theatre still active today, an acting school, writing over twenty full length plays, producing over one hundred, directing many others, playing the drums, becoming a dad. It's not a bad resume for a mentally afflicted human. But the road along the way to all of that, to eventual peace and a tenuous happiness, was hard won.

****

I have been meeting with my brother over Zoom, discussing his relationship to our childhood home life and his emotional challenges. He has lived in California for over fifteen years, and although we visit once a year, this has become our best method of regular communication, even when not addressing this difficult subject. I learned that he spent most of his adolescence, teen years and well into his thirties wrestling with his own depression. He is a therapist himself and believes he may have had a brand of Major Depressive Disorder. He, like me, didn't seek medicinal support until later. In his case he waited until his thirties and, with the exception of some attempts to stop, has remained on medication to this day. He believes that the epilepsy he suffered from his late teens through his twenties (that mercifully ended never to return) was very likely a psychosomatic response to our environment. I am sure he is right. Though he agrees that the big energies and the danger in the home were overwhelming and contributed to his periodically withdrawing energy, it is now clear that what I might have mistaken for a choice to fly under the radar was actually the start of his depression.

Andrew told me that at five years old when crossing the street with our father, he turned and asked him,

"If you knew you were mentally ill, why didn't you tell mom before you were married?"

Quite a statement from a five-year-old. Clearly, the veil of secrecy around Carl's condition had long since dropped by then.

I wouldn't call myself a sickly child, but like Andrew, I got sick a lot too. Many colds and flu kept me out of school. My most ailing year was my sixth when I missed half of the first grade.

Not coincidentally, that was the year right after my brother hit the scene, an attention grab, I am sure. As a newborn, he, understandably, demanded the vast majority of attention. Since the resources were already limited, that piece of the pie felt like almost no attention at all.

My mother was absolutely her best self when one of us was sick. She knew how to lovingly attend. If you were sick, you got what you needed. This, I am sure, was an unconscious motivator to get sick. I contracted appendicitis and mononucleosis during my adolescence and teen years that required long stays at home. My mother's level of attention and care rivaled that of Florence Nightingale.

Not surprisingly, as my psychotherapy proceeded apace, my physical issues started to ease. I still get two or three illnesses a year but nothing that keeps me grounded for long, although increasing age does seem to prolong these bouts. In the last seven years, since I turned fifty-five, conditions of aging have surfaced: sleep apnea (and an intergalactic CPAP machine), tendonitis and a tendon tear (from playing racquetball), arthritis in the lower back and knees, hypoglycemia (controlled by a low sugar diet) and elevated cholesterol (controlled by a statin). Sliding into second head first (I never did that ever again) on the baseball field caused thousands of dollars of dental work (two teeth pulled, two implants), and a lifetime of clenching and grinding from the entire childhood trauma, which therapy hasn't cured, resulting in thousands more, yielding four more extractions and countless crowns... so far. Reflux, which the doctors say comes from lifelong anxiety kept in check by prescription omeprazole, has exacerbated the esophageal stricture... This list reads like issues of an eighty year old, which some days I feel like, especially when I hook myself up to the

CPAP machine for sleep apnea and ingest a daily cocktail of drugs and vitamins. I now own two of those daily medicine holders, one for the morning and one for night, which I use to silently mock when I witnessed my parent's daily intake. I am not mocking anymore.

The one concern that lurks on the edges of my day-to-day existence is life expectancy of those of us with debilitating mental conditions. The average patient lives seven to twelve years shorter than the average human, which puts the projected mortality at sixty-four to sixty-seven-years-old for men. With an eleven-year-old daughter, this is an extremely daunting statistic. I have been physically active and competitive for most of my life. I eat reasonably well. Does this add a few years to those averages? Not so sure. My dad died at sixty-four. I am now sixty-one. What to do with this information? Keep living forward and keep taking the drugs. And try not to dwell on this. Statistics aren't facts, I tell myself.

But the emotional lows and highs have taken a toll on my body. I can feel it. A deep inner fatigue. Some days I feel as vital as when I was in my twenties, more so now because I am less encumbered by the illness. But in still moments, there is often an ache, an exhaustion. Years in the trenches, fighting, fighting. Like a retired football player, except from the inside. I feel it now, and almost every time I am in the middle of a writing session, likely from dredging up old uncomfortable memories, which limits the writing to two hours a day; sometimes, I can push it to three. I feel much better when I do two. After I write, I customarily need a nap to restore my energy.

****

Turns out I also have a milder version of another condition: Misophonia. This term technically means a distaste for sound, but it's an aversion to certain sounds that include but which are not exclusive to loud chewing, slurping of beverages, crinkling of wrappers, tapping of fingers on surfaces. There are many sounds I can tune out (learned amidst the chaos of the early years), but I find these particular sounds unbearable. The acute form of the condition is accompanied by extreme rage and/or panic when triggered. My reaction only reaches a heightened discomfort, impatience, and eventually anger when someone is engaging in one of these behaviors (especially the opening of hard candies during a theatre show) at the expense of others in a public setting. Apparently, in its acute state, people can experience panic attacks or acts of wild rage.

What really caught my eye was the fact that often this condition occurs, not exclusively, but mainly in folks who also suffer from anxiety and depression. That somehow, these sounds are associated with early trauma. It was during those stressful mealtime experiences, a very cramped kitchen table, that I had acute feelings of anxiety and wanted to get away from the table. My mother used to bottle fruit drinks from a pre-mix of powder that would appear at every dinner. One of those glass bottles hit the wall and smashed to pieces during one of those meals. And then there was the moment I recounted earlier when some comment at the dinner table led my father to corner my brother. As we got older, my brother and I could barely get past the table with the ugly plastic white cover with patterns of blue hexagons positioned right next to the cabinet with the griller on top. It was so tight there was only room for one person further down near the stove and sink. This crampedness created the danger of this horrible moment. In that kitchen, I was always in some kind of preparatory readiness. Pleasure, joy, and family bonding were nonexistent in that space.

And then there was the incessant arguing in the last two or three years of my parents' relationship. In my memory, it feels incessant. Of course, like Pavlov proved, raise the expectation of something and you expect it all the time. I went to bed every single night expecting to be awoken by that irrational din.

So sound and trauma are certainly linked.

****

Since the age of eighteen, when I entered therapy, I have been in pursuit of emotional health. I suppose even sanity. The romantic telling of this journey is one of the great spiritual searchers, renegades, and adventurers. Pilgrimages to India, Greece, and Rome. Exciting, thrilling, mind and spirit-altering. But the motive for all of these trips and inner work was to discover solutions to my problems. After my first trip to India, I decided to sponsor an Indian child. I was assigned a lovely, shy young girl, Nagalakshmi, from a small village in the town of Suryapet, two hours east of the big city in the southeast, Hyderabad. That visit with her was life-altering. More on that later.

Those trips offered solace, insight, and a profound understanding of myself and the human condition, but certainly not anything close to a cure. My first Greece trip, when I was twenty-eight, was all about facing staggering fear. The Cuckoo Vai. What the scary, lazy-eyed innkeeper near Delphi called the bird in the adjoining valley that landed on our balcony during the middle of the night. It let out a frightening call like the sound of his/her name. I'm still not sure if such a bird exists or whether it was a bird at all that was on our balcony that night. Later in the Greek trip with my Lena, at the inn outside Meteora (considered, aptly so, one of the wonders of the world. Monasteries built on huge pillar-like remains that once were the banks of a river), where the ouzo-laden Zorba-esque innkeeper looked right at us with a lecherous grin and slapped both his hands together and winked as we made our way to our room. We spent the entire night on the balcony after my girlfriend refused to be held hostage by the metal gates I insisted on closing, temps fast approaching somewhere in the nineties. She invited me out there to face my fear. On that balcony, I finally saw how that underlying fear had run my life. Fear of what? Of everything. Any perceived threat. Anything my mind could conjure. Exacerbated by the occupational hazard of a soon-to-be playwright: a vivid imagination. It didn't help that I was reading Jerzy Kaczynski's masterpiece, The Painted Bird, a macabre fiction about a young boy's misadventures and horrors fleeing the Nazis, loosely based on the author's own experiences. Perfect ground from which my acute paranoia could emerge. I couldn't have scripted better immersion therapy.

The purpose of the trip to India was to explore the Buddha Dharma and take a deeper dive into Hinduism. The trip culminated in an eight-day silent retreat in the Thai monastery in Bodhgaya, the site of Gautama Buddha's enlightenment. In hindsight, the trip itself, traveling solo in this foreign land, was more the actual retreat than sitting silently on a cushion. (To this day, India is the most "foreign" country than any other I have traveled to.) It became a month-long fear-facing immersion. My dad had died that year, and there was also plenty of grieving. It was also magical, intense, and enlightening. I had my earliest experiences of God on that trip. The inexplicable guidance I experienced led me towards magic and away from extreme danger. Guides, teachers, and strangers introduced me to the antidotes of fear- trust, and faith. That introduction opened the door to a lifelong practice of both and also to an ever-deepening letting go of control. On retreat, I also learned and experienced the teachings of impermanence that are bedrock to this day. Good things come and pass, and crises come and go. Cling to nothing, experience the pain, and don't run from it, which I had done for so long. Revel in the joy but cling to nothing. Hard to do. I witnessed mind-blowing events that a kid from a third-story walk up from Queens could never fathom. Immolating bodies, cremated on the banks of the Ganges River in Varanasi (I will never forget the ever-present smell of those burning bodies, inescapable even inside the hotel), Pujas (spiritual/religious rituals) all over the country, sounds of Tablas, indescribable new smells, being a white man in a sea of brown-faced people, cows in the streets, bathing in rivers (where human waste was emptied into), open-air markets on dusty roads, the faces of beaming children, third class trains with peasants who had never seen a white man before. The list goes on and on. Opening myself to India and other cultures around the world has introduced me to the vastness of human experience that no book, movie, or documentary could fully offer. Every trip provided immeasurable gifts. A deeper appreciation of our differences and our connection. And how amazing it was to embrace and celebrate those differences. Try and integrate a bit of them into my own life.

Travel, often driven by spiritual and artistic pursuits, became a vital part of my life. World and national. Those trips seemed to always be a form of medicine, releasing me from my daily home stressors and providing an opening to new and unusual sights, sounds, smells, practices, and beliefs. Incredible nourishment. An addiction I hope to never recover from. I have visited Greece and India twice, Nepal, South Africa, Italy, England several times, Germany, Belize, Mexico, the Dominican Republic, and Canada. And all over the United States.

There is something matchless about experiencing how other people live, getting it off the screen and newsprint and into one's own body. I can never write a play set on foreign soil, overseas or right here in America, without actually going to that place. Even a week or two spent in that country or state makes all the difference.

Artistry aside, travel has changed my life. I refer to it as a stripping of my circuits. Seeing life through a totally different lens. Breathing different air.

****

Long before I entered Alanon's rooms, my late teens and twenties were filled with artificial highs that were an attempt to replace the athletic ones. Alcohol, sex, cocaine, marijuana. Although I was in therapy, I had not yet found the therapist that would change my life. Upon my return home from Branderis, my stepfather referred me to one of his psychiatric colleages. This gentleman, as well-meaning as he was, was also a Freudian. Heady. How on God's green earth could this man of formidable experience have not seen how depressed I was and never discuss medication as an option? There were important moments under his care. Necessary validation. He was the one who told me that it was a miracle that I was still alive after all I had experienced. His care kept me going, but I do not believe he ever significantly altered my healing trajectory. I suppose keeping me alive and semi-functional is not a small thing. I had to become willing and ready to look for a practitioner skilled in helping me get to the deeper roots of my problems. Perhaps my inner world had to collapse even more to feel the impact of therapy's benefit. I was young and learning the language of the inner life.

At the time, those artificial highs were the crutches I needed to get through. One of the important lessons I learned was catalyzed by a close friend's drug use. I came into a session with that first psychiatrist, judging the friend. He challenged my judgment.

"How do you think your friend would get along without the drugs?"

I had to admit that he probably would collapse, or worse. Therapy is hard work. During my long tenure sitting in those offices, I have been asked to feel the unimaginable pain that was buried deep behind those childhood traumas. In the beginning, there was no way I was ready to touch the keg of dynamite living inside of me. I hadn't shed a tear in at least a decade when acting began extracting some. The real waterworks began in my early thirties, and boy, did they come like a dam that finally broke. The effort that went into plugging the breaks all those years must have been enormous, but it was just too dangerous to confront what was living behind it.

Today I recognize those highs as necessary life rafts that many have used (certainly I did at that time) to get through to a place where they won't need that crutch any longer. Actually, I never really liked the substances that much. The taste, the hangovers, the puking. One night, drunk and high in a Nantucket Island bar, I had an epiphany. I was twenty-three. Maybe the first bona fide conscious spiritual experience I ever had. It wasn't a voice or visitation. It was this knowing. That if I didn't quit the substances, I would never figure out/become who I was supposed to be. And then, when pot smoking turned paranoid, and I needed more and more coke to get off, I knew I had to quit. I was twenty-four. I was one of the lucky ones that could stop. Moderate alcohol consumption continued into my early thirties, but then, after receiving the precepts from the Dalai Lama - one of which is ingesting no intoxicants - in a Buddhist Monastery in Kent, New York, I gave up everything. I was finally ready. I began with the therapist who would change my life. With her, I was able to get behind the defenses and feel the pain. Not one artificial intoxicant touched my lips from that moment on until I turned fifty-seven. And since then, in extreme moderation.

The pursuit of sex and women produced my preferred high well into my twenties. I always cast myself as the good guy and led myself to believe I was proceeding respectfully, and never realized the harm I was causing, particularly to myself. I have come to learn and honor the sanctity of the sexual bond and on how many levels it functions. The physical part is delicious, but only part of it. Back then, the heart connection that today is a necessity was lacking. Add to that spiritual and intellectual connection, and you have the makings of a powerful and deeply satisfying sexual relationship.

Ironically, it was that powerful connection that I always craved but was unready to experience. The craving betrayed a strong, persistent longing to be seen, loved, and cared for. All the necessities that were in nonexistent or inconsistent supply in my childhood. I think I believed that if I could get close to a woman sexually all of that would follow. That sexual union would be the portal to a long-term relationship where all those needs would be satisfied. I thought I was ready for that, but I wasn't. This disconnect created much suffering, which is why I got involved with so many unavailable women in my early to mid-twenties. Simulated closeness, but never fully consummated. I see now how terrified I was of being consumed by a woman, not being able to say no, being treated mercurially, conditionally, like my mother treated me. I didn't know any other way. But the hot pursuit of desirable women, even those that offered part-time availability, was exciting and kept the focus off of myself.

In Tibetan Buddhism there is a belief in parallel realities referred to as "realms." Some believe that those realms exist elsewhere. Others think they are all co-existing on this human plane. One of those realms is where the Hungry Ghosts reside - beings whose bellies are infinitely hungry but whose necks are too narrow to eat. So in the process of eating, the food gets stuck and has to be regurgitated. I first heard the concept in a talk given by the late Buddhist Master and Nobel Peace Prize recipient Tich Nat Hanh. The depth of my identification with this manifestation made me weep, for I had experienced this phenomenon both literally and physically.

As I understand it today, the underlying cause of the esophageal stricture that prevents food from passing into my stomach was a physical manifestation, a defense unconsciously designed to effect protection when the organism, my organism, felt threatened. The living, behavioral manifestation became activated when I got close to a woman. I craved love but was terrified to take it in. Big hungry belly, an inability to swallow.

****

There was another vital palliative bridging the gap to the therapy that would finally begin shifting my inner life. After the long, painful college passage to management trainee at

Bloomingdales and then to store manager at Fanny Farmer Candies in the Port Authority (the worst job I have ever had), I escaped to a job on Nantucket island. It was at the end of that long summer that I cooked up a harebrained scheme to take another crack at pre- med. I convinced myself that somehow all the debauchery (and that summer had plenty) was the cause for my failure the first time around at Brandies University. To my complete amazement, I was accepted into the Columbia five-year medical program. I returned to New York with a renewed sense of purpose which quickly evaporated. After two weeks, I dropped out. My best option at the time was to go back to work for my cousin. It was at that point, an absolute early career bottom, that I prostrated myself to the universe. I had no clue what I wanted to do and, more relevantly, who I was. I did not consider myself a God person before this moment. I was embracing spirituality, practicing Transcendental Meditation regularly, and had that spiritual epiphany on the island about the drinking. Not only had I never really contemplated God in a serious way, but the mention of the word brought up aversion.

Dad always professed a deep connection to God. There were periods when he wrapped Tefillin, leather bands wrapped around the arm and head with a small a box containing prayers that get placed on the worshipper's forehead. This is an ancient Jewish ritual practiced mainly by conservative and orthodox Jews. And then, one day, the entire practice stopped, never to return again. I wonder if that had something to do with an increasingly futile struggle with his mental illness. Feeling abandoned by God. For a long time, I associated the Divine with his insanity and ran in the opposite direction. In recent years, I have come to appreciate the rare wave length Dad was plugged into. An insurmountable divide separates most people from a connection with God. Today, I believe that there is some form of genuine, albeit intermittent, contact with an unseen realm that my father's unique circuitry permitted him. He also was severely schizophrenic, so it was hard to discern which messages he thought he was receiving were illusions and which had more substance. There was a distinct tonal difference between his hallucinogenic states and his clairvoyant ones. The latter did not arise with any other symptoms of his disease. Easy to write those off, herding those "leadings" in with the rest of the others. Once my fear around my dad had begun to abate I started seeing those moments differently.

Back in the midst of that early career desperation, I still had no conscious connection to God, nor did I seek one. I needed answers, so I opened myself up to guidance. What began to arrive seemed so completely unlikely that it could have been easy to discount. The first person to suggest acting to me was a dear Bloomingdales friend who was an actor himself. He suggested I meet with his coach, which I evaded until I started dating another Bloomingdale employee who was also an actress whose career shortly thereafter took off. Before she left for a job in Italy, she encouraged me to try. Then a family member who had embraced acting later in life offered the same encouragement, recommending other great teachers to study with. To understand the oddity of this, one must consider my relationship with theatre when I was younger. When I auditioned for *Swiss Family Robinson* at the age of ten, my singing voice was so bad that I got stuck in a bit non singing roles for the rest of the musicals presented through sixth grade. I would have run as far away from the theatre as possible, but participation was obligatory. In junior high, I avoided anything to do with the theatre, and in high school, the closest I came to the stage was ogling from a distance at the pretty girls in the drama club. When I was seated next to any of them in class, I froze from intimidation. In light of those experiences, these suggestions to my twenty-one-year-old self as a potential path seemed meant for someone else. But I couldn't ignore these three random acts of unsolicited encouragement. I felt so lost and desperate that I agreed to try my friend's acting coach and enter an acting class.

I stepped into my first class at HB (Herbert Berghof) Studios in Manhattan and, before very long, was drawn in. Not initially as a career choice, but definitely as a serious study. It wasn't the imaginative part of the craft that drew me, it was the premium placed on truth, truthful moments, and truthful responses. What the heck did that even mean? In my home, the truth was too frightening. It was meant to remain hidden. But there was something inside me that knew that these truths needed to be exhumed. And this place, this craft, was inviting me to do so.

The lay understanding of acting lies far from the truth of it. A student once told me that after taking a year of class, she felt like she occupied "more of herself." I completely identify with that. Acting introduces or re-introduces one to the inner panoply of emotions, fears, repressed dreams, and needs. A very scary proposition for most. Some of that raw material is hard to get to, but the incessant drumbeat of the acting class, not loud, not urgent, but persistent, inevitably moves one in that direction. As actors, we need to empathize with our characters' inner workings, which requires understanding and empathy for ourselves. Without the connections to our own inner life, good acting becomes nearly impossible. For instance, if you are being asked to act as a character whose primary challenge in the play or film is betrayal, you, as the actor, need to be fully in touch with the ways you have been betrayed. If access to that is blocked, then you wouldn't be able to take on that role. For this reason and others, acting is one of the most courageous professions. Who among us has the capacity and desire to face ourselves this way? The immersion never ceases. There are unchartered corners of our psyches that always need more exploration.

It was a slow process, chipping away at the calcification protecting my emotional life. This acting landscape was the first frontier of my inner rediscovery. It was incredibly hard but I began a lifelong journey.

The acting craft, I know, motivated me to find a better therapist, one who would encourage me to dig deeper. That person was recommended by an old camp friend who was herself a therapist.

My friend knew I was artistic and needed something a bit more out of the box. Carol, this new practitioner, specialized in a body- based therapy called Core Energetics. An offshoot of Bioenergetic therapy, this practice focuses on understanding and softening the emotional body armor. I had never heard of this therapy before, which didn't much matter to me. I did know that I had an esophageal issue, which wasn't really getting any better. Maybe this kind of body-based therapy could help. And body armor, I had plenty. The forerunner of these two approaches was Wilhelm Reich, the founder of body-based therapies. He believed that a skilled professional could diagnose the client's emotional holdings by studying their bodies. Parakis and Lowen were the Jung and Freud of this lineage of therapy. Parakis' Core departure from Lowen's Bio Energetics (just like Jung's from Freud) was the acknowledgment of life's spiritual component and the need to invite that into the healing process.

I spent close to fifteen years with this Carol. She accelerated my opening process, which, of course, helped my acting, but more relevantly, helped heal the darker wounds of my life. I didn't know I possessed that many tears. I would cry so violently at times that I would begin to vomit. I learned that in this deep healing, the vomiting response was quite common; so much hurt, so many abuses internalized. Carol, my first and most important of a few great female therapists, most certainly became a surrogate for my mother. Transference is a common therapeutic occurrence, but this was more than that. This was receiving the attention and the validation that I had never truly received from my own mother, not until much later in her life. Just that consistent, unwavering, skilled female attention and love provided a huge healing in itself.

****

After I started with my therapist and just before starting Alanon, I met the woman who would be my first truly serious and important relationship.

Lena and I met at the small theatre I co-ran in NoHo (North of Houston in Manhattan) in 1990. She was auditioning for a role in an early Harold Pinter play I was performing in called *The Collection.* She was beautiful and gifted and if instant love is possible, I fell in love at first meet. As one of the producers, I "urged" the director to cast her. (Not the first producer to urge a director to cast an actor) The challenge was that we didn't have any scenes together, so we never rehearsed at the same time. Sometimes our rehearsals were back to back, so we did get some brief time to get to know each other.

It was during one of those back-to-backs, where we began to run large chunks of the play that we really got acquainted. There was instant chemistry. But- she was married. I had spent my twenties in too many third-wheel situations and was not interested in getting involved in another one, especially with a married woman. I took her to lunch and explained this to her. I told her that I could most certainly fall in love with her and likely already had, but I just couldn't go there with her. Then the usual blah, blah about if she was available down the road, and so on. Two days later, at our next rehearsal, she announced that she just left her husband.

Who expects an outcome like this? Maybe in the most fantastical Disney or Hallmark movie, but not in actual life. Perhaps the biggest shock of my life and one that changed the course of it. Higher Power intervening. So many positive life changes came of out this wonderful relationship. Being introduced to Buddhism, which led to a decade of practice and two trips to India, validation by her and her theatre family that I was on the right path, an introduction to the man who would become my artistic mentor and eventually life as a playwright. I am fairly confident in saying that the positive changes were mutual. She had been an actress, one play in particular that had an impact on the theatre scene and her career. She was gifted, but she grew progressively weary of the life of an actor and the entire theatre gestalt, having lived in it since she was born. During our time together, she went back to college and made the leap into fiction writing. She is now a respected fiction writer and teacher. Not the least of these influences was her support in attending Alanon and doing whatever it took to solve my inner turmoil. I spent a week at a quality addiction rehab in a family program, went on many therapeutic retreats, and countless Buddhist teachings, many she attended with me. It was a time of great growth and great self- acceptance. But though I believed that I had or was overcoming my darkness after each run of big work, I was still wrestling with my scoured inner life when our romantic relationship came to an end. We remain dear friends.

Creating in theatre has been therapeutic, certainly the visceral practice of acting, but, alas, not the cure. If only it were, I would have been cured many times over. Writing plays remains a cathartic one, but without the tiny pills I was eventually prescribed, I would find no lasting peace. But, I believe this journey through Alanon, Buddhism, theatre, the relationship with Lena and then Lois, led me to a place where I could embrace who I was, in all of my beauty and illness, and finally accept the medical solution that I had so long railed against but desperately needed.

****

The architecture of a depressive episode.

I flew to Nepal by way of India to visit my then-long-term girlfriend, Lois. She was at the tail end of a thirteen-month spiritual-artistic journey in the East. We, or more honestly, I, decided that we should separate during this period. We were having problems, and more and more, I felt the pressure of her necessity to have a child. This year would provide the space I needed to live with this question and see what absence and freedom would do to me.

Before she left, I had committed to monthly Skype calls and a trip to the East to visit her. I had been sponsoring a child in India, Nagalakshmi, for a decade, and this would provide me with the opportunity to visit her, spend time in the south of India, and then fly to Nepal for ten days to visit my maybe-still-girlfriend before coming home.

My sort of ex was tremendously sad and angry that I had made this decision. I was compassionate, but knew it was the necessary choice, at least for me. Eventually, our calls became more relaxed and loving, albeit tinged with hurt and sadness.

I was still uncertain what the fate of our relationship would be, but I was committed to honoring my promise of traveling to see her.

The visit to Nagalakshmi was extraordinary. She lived in a village called Suryapet, an hour east of the city of Hyderabad. I was treated like a visiting dignitary, which was startling and completely unexpected and a peak life experience. I was adorned with handmade flowered wreaths, regaled with music and dance, and given a tour of the vibrant village with a sea of beautiful children beaming up at me. Though I was sponsoring one child, the monthly donation actually went toward the well-being of the entire village, so they all came out to show their appreciation. Sitting with Nagalakshmi and her family was surreal, having only conversed through letters for ten years. She was a shy girl, but the affection we shared was palpable. At one moment during our conversation, under a thatched sitting area, she went into her house (their dwelling for three, not much bigger than the sitting area) and came out with a stack of ribboned letters; every communication we had had over all of those years. I was blown away. There is a photo of her and me sitting in that thatched enclosure on that steaming hot day (attendants from the organization followed me around with water waiting for the first sign of me passing out), her wiping a red bindi- a dot of red powder- from my brow with a towel, a towel they gave me to take home, that was dripping down my forehead. She had placed the bindi upon my head after we first arrived. This was such an intimate and loving moment between two relative strangers. It was a moment I will never forget.

After an incredible day, a day which felt like a month, I was brought back to my hotel room in Hyderabad. Once alone, I wept. I wept for a long time. I am still not certain what the weeping was about, but I suspect it had something to do with the prospect of having a child or not having one, activated by the kids in the village. I was still, at that time, holding fast to my child-rearing ambivalence.

After a Yoga retreat in Trivandrum, at the southern tip of the country, I flew north to Nepal. The long escalator down to the passenger pickups remains indelible. At the very bottom, my girlfriend Lois stood awaiting me. Within minutes I could tell how her time overseas had grounded her, clearly catalyzed by her Buddhist practices. This was the woman that I had fallen in love with. The fantasy of this romantic reunion drew to its end at the bottom of the escalator when she revealed that she had a boyfriend who she was in love with, who graciously was "sitting a meditation retreat" to give us space. Wow. There was no rule against dating during our time apart, but how about telling me before I fly halfway around the world to see her? She was clearly still quite angry and hurt by my need to separate. I remained, but with more inner protection than previously planned. It's not an awesome portend.

I was sitting in a Nepalese internet café, a lifeline to anyone anywhere who is traveling out of the States, particularly in Asia, for a lengthy session processing this arrival news with my friends, when I felt a tap on my shoulder. I turned. It was a vision. An incredibly beautiful woman offered me a cookie. No, I am not inventing this. It actually happened just that way. Of course, I accepted the overture and we sat there eating cookies and chatting. Turned out that she had just come out of the northern Nepal mountains, having worked in an orphanage. My kind of woman. At the end of this lengthy encounter, I knew I had an option- follow her into the horizon or remain committed to my visit and purpose. Though that moment haunted me with 'what-ifs' for quite a while (a moment that was the impetus for a play I wrote), and now hardly at all (having an amazing child can do that), I made the choice to stay the course with Lois.

My time in Nepal was wonderful, brutal, and confusing. There was such joy on both our parts, I think, to see each other, hang out, laugh and reconnect about all that mattered. Spiritual pursuit was a high priority for us both and to experience her new discovery of Tibetan Buddhism in a historic Tibetan Buddhist center was thrilling. The experience included circumambulations around the Boudhanath Stupa (a large Tibetan flag-adorned cone- like edifice in the middle of the town square), visits to the monastery and the art school where she was learning Buddhist Thangka painting, and roaming her haunts all around this Buddhist-centric universe. Boudhanath in Kathmandu became one of the two Tibetan Buddhist epicenters received graciously by the Nepalese after their exile from Tibet (the other Dharamsala in Northern India). I had always viewed the Tibetans as the Catholics of Buddhism: lots of ritual, imagery, and deity worship. They are the only Buddhist sect that puts deity imagery right in the middle of practice. To be fair, these deities function more as manifestations of energies and not actual gods, but they are still the focus of many meditational prayer and prostration practices. I was committed to a much more austere Buddhist practice and lineage, so this visit opened me up to an entirely other side of Buddhism. I was always thrilled by the way, as an artist, Lois saw the world and how it opened up my seeing both inner and outer. But on this visit, the new dude was very present in her heart. Perhaps I should have, but I didn't get my own hotel room after learning of her romantic news. Instead, I stayed in a spare room in her apartment. I am still an athlete, after all, and always up for healthy competition. But we were able to get to know each other anew and unromantically since sex was off the table that week, which, although frustrating, was also probably a benefit. An underlying agenda was to investigate whether we wanted (at some point down the line) to continue as a couple. This lack of sexuality helped clarify that. It was intimate. Lots and lots of laughs, which had always been our flagship, and even some stolen kisses. I took a five day trek by myself in the lower Annapurna range of the Himalayas, an experience which was equal parts dumb and breathtaking. I was nowhere near in shape to take on the daily climbing that was required of me but somehow manifested my athletic self and rose to the occasion. I came off that mountain probably in the best shape of my life. After the trek, we spent more time together, and then I headed home, still not knowing what the future of our relationship would hold.

Shortly after I arrived home, I realized three things almost simultaneously: In the year apart, Lois had undergone profound change, there was a pretty good chance that we would never get back together again, and I was still very much in love with her. The next shoe to drop was learning a day or so later that the space my acting school and our theatre had been renting for our classes and workshops was being sold to another organization, and we had only a few months to leave. Almost simultaneously, my dear friend and managing director of the theatre, Nate, announced he was leaving.

Emotional pile on. It is not good for anyone but worse for

someone who suffers from depression. Any one of those things would be very hard to deal with but taken together, they sent me into a tailspin. Amidst that crisis, I kept it together and steered the organization to a new space. Miraculously members of our board of directors found money to pay a new managing director. One of the skills I developed as a kid was crisis clarity and execution. And after the smoke cleared, I crashed.

When I fall into a depression, nothing that I love provides the slightest bit of pleasure. I recently learned there is a medical term for this. It's a condition called Anhedonia associated with depressive episodes. To drag myself out of bed was hard enough each day. Getting through the day, leading the organization, teaching classes, and even writing became a Sisyphean task. Somehow, with great effort, I managed to get to the other side. Slowly the joy of daily life returned. From start to finish, this was a four-month process. It felt a lot longer. Days that used to fly by moving as slow as dripping molasses.

****

Is depression behavioral or organic? I wrestled with this question for years, often railing at the medical profession for overmedicating my father. They say that alcoholics have a disease, an allergy. They have one drink and can't stop at one. But I know from years in those rooms that that is only one part of it. There is also the ground from which that allergy emerges. The childhood. The lack of adequate nurturance. My dad had a very difficult childhood. His mom, my favorite grandmother seemed tame enough except for the time she purposefully let my dad's dog leap out of the first-floor window, never to be seen again (my father told that story many times as an adult). But it was my grandfather. The punishing, competitive, jealous father

111

that tilled the soil for my dad's struggles. Grandpa Lou was a man of two lives. In his young adult life he was a star loomsman for the then nascent Burlington Mills, whose factories at the time were located in New York City. It was when the company relocated to Philadelphia that the trouble began for Lou. He was one of a few that the company asked to go to Philly. His mother and father, émigrés from Rumania and Russia, would not permit their son to leave the nest. And in those days most Jewish immigrant children placed loyalty over destiny. Is it an act of loyalty to sabotage one's own joy? Loyalty to whom, to what? Lou betrayed his own dream, and one he had worked very hard to achieve. He stayed in New York with his family and shifted from a world of esteem to the life of a plumber. A respectable and well-compensated trade for sure, but a far cry from the life he was living and the career he loved. At Burlington he was respected, producing beautiful fabric, always looking dapper in photographs, proud. Contrast that with the photos of him years later. Dour. Angry. My father was his only son and the primary recipient of all of this regret and jealousy of my father's more promising future. Life and its tragedies. His father's inability to relate to him, to show him any affection and love was a huge one for my dad. And in some way that tragedy was handed down along to me and my brother. Not the absence of love and affection. My father could express that in abundance. It was the impact of Lou's treatment of him that informed, in his worst moments, how he treated us.

But would Carl have become schizoid effective (the most recent diagnosis for schizophrenia coupled with bipolar disorder) with even the most loving and supportive home life? Would it have reared its head with such severity? Would other parents have noticed the signs of this earlier on and gotten him help? If they had recognized my father's charisma and Frank Sinatra baby blues, coupled with a sonorous voice, and allowed him to tour Europe fronting his army band after his tour of duty was over, would that have altered my dad's trajectory? Instead, Lou sentenced my father to the same fate that he was bound to. (My grandparents seemed to covet the Rosenthal china my father had purchased in Germany over his happiness and purpose.) We will never know. And I am not sure that science ever will, either. But it's hard to believe that the severity of his illness wasn't affected by nurture in some measure. In fact, that is the conventional wisdom of the day. Take the prescribed medicine and, by God, stay in therapy.

****

The trajectory of all of my depressions follows a similar path: fear that moves into overwhelming fear and anxiety followed by an adrenal shutdown, listlessness, the above-mentioned anhedonia (the sapping of all joy from every pursuit I loved), difficulty, and then an inability to get out of bed in the morning, and then finally and inevitably, suicidal thoughts. Before I acquiesced to chemical help, I did what I knew how to do in response- thrust myself deeper into therapy. Cry out the wound, or so I thought. In those days, I was convinced that the arrival of the depression was a sign that I had more inner work to do and that I hadn't bled the many childhood wounds dry yet. To accelerate the process, I increased the weekly frequency of the Alanon meetings and therapy sessions, signed up for weekend "mat trips" (primal scream-esque retreats) with my therapist, and ramped up my Buddhist practice. That was the regimen. It seemed to have worked any number of times. What I didn't know then was that the cycles, for me, did organically come to an end. Did all this work hasten the natural cycle?

I have come to believe that the answer to whether these depressive episodes were brought on genetically or environmentally is- both. A predisposition that is activated by a pile-on of real or imagined crises.

****

That a tiny pill, as big as or smaller than a raisin, can completely balance my brain remains an incredibly humbling notion. And also terrifying. What if, like in my father's case, it stops working? What if, when traveling, I lose the pills? Thank God neither has happened, but living with these possibilities never escapes me. I am now dependent.

As critical as all those years of therapy, sitting on the cushion meditating, the many hours logged in Alanon had been, their benefits began to wane. Although they remain a major part of the overall "recovery plan," they cannot alter the underlying brain chemistry sufficiently. And I was getting older- then forty-five- my will to fight was waning. I was exhausted and scared. My belief that enough therapy, enough spiritual realization, would beat these cycles had finally turned. I faced the fact that I likely needed more help. Crawling into the psychiatrist's office was the white flag moment. I had been running and fighting for so long, holding fast to the belief that I would not become my father. I hadn't become him, but with the doctor that day, I learned that I suffered from a mental disorder and needed a pill just like him, perhaps more than one. That was a really hard day. On the one hand, I walked out of the pharmacy, hopeful that I was holding the solution. On the other, I had to submit to the fact that I had a disease. As already mentioned: Major Depressive Disorder. I suffered from this all along, just didn't know the name before that first office visit. It sounded ominous. It is. It

114

took me quite a while to accept that I was harboring the hope that this was temporary and that hope was a fantasy. The other thing about antidepressants: they take a month or so to kick in, which is why I was also prescribed Klonopin. The movie "Silver Linings Play Book" did a disservice to this drug, representing it as one that produces wild and intense side effects. Perhaps these do occur in some cases, but never to me. Klonopin saved my ass. It is short- acting (it kicks in immediately) anti-anxiety medicine, which also slakes the effects of depression. Without that drug, I would have spent weeks in deep depression before the SSRI (selective serotonin reuptake inhibitor) kicked in.

Here's another fact: Medicine can manage the symptoms of the disease, but it cannot cure it. This means there is a life impact, like the one I outlined above, where the external circumstance and the internal chemical response can overwhelm the impact of the drugs. As I have gotten deeper into this recovery there are signs that typically precede the onset of an episode. Fear that amplifies to anxiety, to extreme anxiety. If I don't head this off at the pass with enough Klonopin with an increased dosage of Celexa, then my system starts shutting down, and lethargy sets in. Then there is no way of slaking the avalanche. Sometimes the Klonopin and the increase in the dosage of the antidepressant can head it off or at least lessen the impact. The increased dose can and does, over time, catch up to the force of the internal chemistry and tame it. But that can take several grueling, torturous months.

This disease needs to be watched closely and managed. I am fortunate to have a brilliant and caring psychiatrist who knows me and my cycles well enough to make the needed adjustments. Through careful observation, she has concluded that my episodes often, but not always, get triggered when the days get shorter and there is increasingly less sunlight. But it doesn't matter what the seasons are when the circumstantial pile-ons happen, and, in my experience, no antidepressant is powerful enough to completely arrest the chain reaction that leads down the rabbit hole. The duration of the darkness is hastened by the medicine, but they are not usually preventative.

****

A former student embarked on a highly risky venture of opening up his own theatre in New Paltz, New York. I was asked to provide some tips. The theatre opened and immediately met with success. I saw several plays that first season, and although the quality varied, the work was generally very good. In the second season, he invited me to see the first offering, and of course, I went. It was a one-woman show, written by a man, with much audience participation, about a daughter living with a suicidal mother and facing her own depression. I was glad that my friend was giving this subject matter much-needed exposure. This was the kind of theatre I had produced at my own theatre and have been committing to writing: relevant and provocative. But within minutes of the play starting I found myself uncomfortable. The performance felt shtick-laden and disingenuous as if the intensity of the subject matter was so difficult that the actor's emotional separation from the subject matter would make it more accessible to the audience. I left the theatre not knowing whether this actress had any personal relationship to suicide or depression. I felt let down, not only by the performance but by my friend, who I expected to recognize this lack of authenticity. It is true, in his defense, that once in production, the artistic director loses less and less control short of canceling the show, which is never an option for a small not-for-profit theatre.

The only real insight that was communicated on stage was the daughter's self-acceptance and mom-acceptance, but I was so alienated by the heavy-handed humor that this conclusion seemed trite and unearned. Folks seemed to enjoy it. The actress did work awfully hard, and she was likable. Everyone rose to their feet at the end except me. But people will rise to their feet in theatre as if they have watched Marlon Brando or Meryl Streep in every performance they attend. If a few stand, everyone else feels obligated to follow. Which is why standing ovations are unofficially outlawed in British theatre. Now, I recognize that I am tough. I make and teach theatre for a living and treat it like a religion. The way religion was intended to be treated. Reverentially. A matter of life and death. Salvation. Not the standard that most attendees bring to the theatre. Entertainment and interest are often sufficient enough. I always aim for catharsis and transformation or at least an experience that sets that as its destination. Suicide is an incredibly personal topic for my family. My father tried to kill himself three times, which made me much more than a theatergoer that night or even a theatre professional sitting and watching. I am usually the toughest critic in the house. That night the play and performance had to pass through the eye of a needle.

What this play never mentioned is that when a person attempts suicide, even for attention-seeking purposes, their life becomes unbearable. Who would reject this glorious precious life, throw it all away? Only the ones whose lives have become utterly unlivable. Even my dad, who experienced life that way a lot of the time, didn't actually go all the way. He knew someone would be home and must have known that the doses he took were likely not enough to actually kill him. Yet, the message was clear. He was miserable, and he wanted everyone to know: my mother, us kids, his parents and my mother's parents, his doctors, the entire psychiatric profession, and a world that had no true understanding or acceptance of him. I am not sure that any of his attempts ever brought him the intended measure of understanding from anyone on this list. No one can ever know what it's like until, God forbid, they are living inside of it. That degree of suffering was never communicated in that play. And the process or solutions towards achieving acceptance weren't even glanced at.

****

There are angels out there. When I move towards help, even just a few inches, gifted, caring people have appeared. Doctors, therapists, an abundance of amazing friends, and members in the rooms of Alanon. I tell my students that there is a huge difference between compassion and empathy. Most of us, unless we are cruel, selfish, or narcissistic, feel sorrow or sadness when we learn that someone is going through a bad time. Compassion doesn't require a huge leap. But empathy necessitates walking in the other person's shoes, which either requires a profound imagination, which most folks don't possess, or having experienced some related crisis. There is something about sharing with someone who totally gets what you are going through that is powerful medicine, even magic. It's one of the purest reasons, I think, that the twelve-step rooms work so well. Being around fellow sufferers. And slowly, imperceptibly, something begins to shift. The thinking shifts and the feeling of uselessness, of hopelessness, lifts. And one day it's as if it was all a dream.

I need to reinforce something. Without the medicine, I'm not sure I would still be here. I am one of the lucky ones. According to John's Hopkins, thirty percent of people who suffer from Major Depressive Disorder have what is called Treatment-resistant depression. In short, these folks do not respond to antidepressants. I am fortunate to be in that seventy percent who does. Since it is a cyclical disease, I am certain most of these folks eventually pull out of it. My dad was, most of the time— one of the thirty percenters. But he had a different disease than I, and I am certain those statistics- especially in the sixties and seventies- when the science was still relatively nascent, and he was in his acute phase, were much worse. The three times he attempted to kill himself, my mother found him, and then emergency rooms pumped his stomach of the pills he had swallowed. Something tells me that if he was really serious, he would have selected a different time frame or place so as not to be discovered. But who can be sure? When the pain was too unbearable, maybe he needed to disappear in that moment, no more waiting. An abundance of lethal pills were always available to him.

There are tranquilizers that are fast-acting and do take the pain away temporarily; this is why so many folks who suffer from mental illness drink or do drugs. It's a fast escape. But sadly, it doesn't last long, and things are most often worse when the effects of the substance wane.

Deep in the depressive hole is a dark place. I have already listed these side effects: Hopeless, helpless, a deadening, living inside quicksand, being pulled forever downward. A sense that this feeling will never end. Still, all of that feels like an insufficient description. It's the worst feeling I have ever known. And at the bottom of that hole, the inevitable impulse for escape is suicide. We are organisms that fight to the death to preserve ourselves, so things must have to get pretty bad to consider that final option. But that option remains. I don't say that blithely or with any intent to carry it out. But living in that without end is no life at all. I have a friend who also suffers from the same disease who does not respond or whose improvements are short-lived. She spends her life careening from long depressions to hypomanic periods. I haven't asked her about suicidal ideations, but it's hard to believe that she doesn't wrestle with them.

If the drugs stopped working and I were sentenced to long periods in an endless abyss, what would I do? When a dear therapist asked me if I could pledge never to take my own life, I couldn't do it. Pledging that meant accepting a life lived in that hopeless, joyless, loveless place. Many have made that ultimate choice. We know some of their names; folks in the spotlight: Phillip Seymour Hoffman, Robin Williams, Spalding Grey. Can anyone fathom what they were going through before they made that choice? They all had loving families, children, and bountiful careers, yet, they still took this step.

My commitment to myself to my daughter, and the legacy of my family is that I will vigorously seek every possible remedy before that ever becomes a real option. I have thought about suicide, sometimes seriously, when I am in those seemingly endless dark places, but even there, I have never taken actual steps in that direction. I hope never to have to consider that.

****

When my ex-wife Lois and I first met, we were deeply in love. I was thirty-seven, and she was twenty-five. It wasn't just the sexual chemistry, though, that was a vital part of our relationship. It was the deep connection that was apparent to both of us. It took us a year and a half to come together as a couple, as we both had partners when we first met.

After my long spiritual search, I found the Quakers, the Religious Society of Friends. It combined my newfound belief in God with the quiet practice of meditative silence. It became another refuge for me on the journey towards recovery. There was this day when I was feeling particularly confused about my then relationship with Lena and walked into the Quaker meeting house and there was Lois. Sitting there in silence, beautiful, and in my romanticized version, she was wrapped in this peaceful and angelic light. I was instantly smitten. In retrospect, Lois and my relationships with our then partners were on their last legs, but we both remained true to our partners. That didn't stop us from having lunches together after Quaker worship and finding that we had central passions in common: art-making and spiritual discovery. She was and is a fine artist and former actress, and of course, I was deeply ensconced in the theatre world. Our deep talks about theatre rekindled her interest in acting, and soon enough, she was taking classes at my acting studio. It was clear very early that her being my student was not a good idea, so I asked my colleague to work with her.

A year or so after we met we both ended our relationships with our partners and began dating. Soon thereafter, I invited her into the acting ensemble of the theatre. Lois is gifted in all of her artistic pursuits. Painting, sculpting, poetry, stop motion animation and also acting. That became abundantly clear once she joined the ensemble. This, of course, allowed us more time together and led to a number of years of exciting theatre collaboration, followed by her rigorous investigation as an artist, experimenting with the various forms mentioned above. It was soon clear that acting wasn't the perfect vehicle for her art, and settled on fine art, the original form she had studied at Brown and the Rhode Island School of Design. By the time we met, I had spent nearly two decades in self-discovery and supported her work on herself in every way I could. I was also exploring a new landscape creatively- playwriting- which quickly became the central form of my artistic pursuits. And she was equally supportive of this new journey.

What went wrong?

When we finally got married, I was forty-seven, and she was thirty-five. Upon our return from Nepal, we entered couples therapy, seemingly worked through our issues, and recommitted to our love and working through whatever new issues might arise. The problem was that strong day-to-day habits established over the first ten years of our relationship proved extremely hard to break.

The other crucial detail of our story is that from the start, we had been there for each other's brokenness. We each became a fixer of the other. I had been in Alanon seven years when we met, seventeen when we got married, and thought I had grown past that compulsion. Clearly, I hadn't. It became harder and harder to live together, each of us feeling judged by the other. Even love that becomes impossible, damaging, and impractical can be too compelling to let go of. And after we were married for two years, Olivia Meyer arrived. Neither Lois nor I knew at the time that the relationship was already beyond repair. We were glorying in the arrival of our beautiful girl. Our relationship could temporarily take a back seat to our issues. But the soil had already been sewn with too many resentments. Care and support for each other gave way to a lack of trust and self-protection.

****

My dad had a common-law wife he met in his last long outpatient stint at St. Vincent's in Harrison, New York. She suffered from depression, bad enough to need a protracted outpatient term. My dad had become a lifer. He was in that program until his Parkinson's prevented him from walking. Their relationship lasted ten years. She got better. My dad got worse. My dad's dual diagnosis of schizoid affective disease and Parkinson's disease was too much for her. The medical consensus was that the many years of psychotropic medication had worn out his nervous system. Very sad, but without them, his life would likely have ended much sooner, or he would have become a permanent resident at a mental facility. Initially, I blamed her for abandoning my dad in the middle of his time of worst need, the Parkinson's growing worse and worse. In truth, my dad's time of worst need was his entire life, at least from the point of his first nervous breakdown at thirty-two.

Remember, we did learn that my father was engaged to another woman before my mom. Our best guess is that she either learned about or witnessed an early bout of his mental illness and decided that this life wasn't for her. Who knows what her story was, what she was afflicted with, if anything. One of the greatest pieces of street wisdom from an AA friend and warrior: "Two sickies don't make a welly." My dad's relationships. My marriage.

I need to find a welly. I am hoping that Lois does, too. Let's face it, no one is totally well, but is finding someone who does not share in the same unwellness as me too much to ask? Have I grown enough to attract another who has grown as well? I hope so. I love companionship. I love women. I like aloneness but hate loneliness. I adored my daughter, six, when Lois and I separated. I hate that she is a child of divorce, but I do know that we will be modeling a healthy choice for her, which now features happier, more peaceful home environments. In Alanon, they say that in the height of our disease, we don't date we take hostages. No more hostage-taking for me, I swear. On some level, Lois and I took each other as hostages even though that taking and being taken felt so sweet from the start. Loving, devoted, destined, soul connected. All true. But sadly, emotional hostages- to each other and also to our pasts.

This hostage-taking of my early adulthood feels like it was rooted in longing for what I didn't receive in adequate portions as a kid from my mother – unconditional attention, admiration, curiosity of who I was and was becoming, respect for my humanness, and apology when something was said or done that was destructive to me. I craved all of this from a woman. I searched for that clumsily, sloppily, and often from the wrong people. Beauty was and always has been an elixir and also a blinder. And when the woman of substance seemed to appear, I would get committed way too quickly, often move into their place or to have them move in with me way too soon. I don't want to invalidate the real attractions and the very real connections that I had with the meaningful women in my life. However, I had no patience. There were plenty of very strong hormones running rampant within me at that time, but also this craving that I sometimes still feel around women whom I have a connection. There is this song by Hosier called "Someone New," which speaks to meeting someone every day who he falls in love with "just a little bit." I get that. Is that natural? Is it particular to me and those like me who my astrologer claims are governed by Uranus (independence) and Neptune (beauty, fantasy). I imagine that is true in part. But I have also spent many years being governed by what Alanon calls the "God-shaped hole." That perennially dissatisfied side of us needs to be fed, satisfied, and filled but cannot be filled by any other human.

As I have gotten older, I am less and less directed by hormones or by the seeping wounds (which have undergone a lot of healing). But for many years jumping in and trying to care for, help heal, or even save someone, or have them do the same for me, felt like love. I am not used to falling for someone who is completely available and also has her shit together. I have been studying all of this closely since my separation and subsequent divorce. When I am able to get beyond the horniness for an attractive woman, it's amazing how few of them I really want to get deeply involved with. One therapist has said that because of my unique combination of priorities (theatre making, writing, spiritual pursuit, and raising a young child) there aren't a lot of good matches for me. My other therapist is convinced that love and connection can develop over time. This is completely counterintuitive to how I have operated. If I felt it instantly it was somehow realer. But I am bringing much more suspicion to that instantaneous feeling. I am getting much better at taking time to get to know a woman so I can ascertain whether we are a good fit. Whether we can truly satisfy each other's primary needs. I am still fairly convinced that that X factor appears rather quickly. Am I still addicted to the high of intense romance, or is this just how I am built? As they say, more will be revealed.

****

My father died in 1997, just before my thirty-fifth birthday. His dying process was as difficult and tragic as the entirety of his life.

He finally succumbed to Parkinson's disease but not before

being fully rehabilitated at the fantastic Burke Rehabilitation Center in Westchester. He entered the facility with legs that would seize up after walking ten steps. He would literally be frozen in the standing-up position until the legs would relax, and he could proceed a few more steps until this happened again. The prototypical Parkinson's patient we are all familiar with is the one who shakes. Think of Katherine Hepburn or Michael J. Fox. But there is another class of patients that suffer from the seizing of their limbs. My father left Burke three weeks after being admitted, practically skipping down the street. He looked and seemed fully healed. But then there was the aftercare. He had been given a slew of exercises that his home aid could not get him to do. The rest was predictable. He went from an assisted living facility to a nursing home, then for a stint at the mental institution, and finally back to a different nursing home completely unable to walk. Of course, it was his 34-year-old son (moi) who found and then arranged his admission to these facilities.

A call came into my phone, which I missed. It was the hospital he had been rushed to after his lung collapsed. I was his healthcare proxy, and they wanted to get direction about resuscitation before they hooked him up to life support. I don't know what I would have done if I had actually received the call. Who wants to make that kind of decision for anybody, especially a parent?

My father was intubated and quickly fell into a coma. He lived out the last nine months with the support of the breathing machine. Nine months. Why? One of the traumas of living with a mentally ill parent is never receiving the attention and care you need. This leads to the desire to fix or cure so that their health is restored (this pattern followed me into love relationships as described above.) Consciously, the healing intention is for their own good. Unconsciously there was deeper motivation - if my dad was healthy enough, then maybe he could finally provide the full complement of parenting I needed. When my dad felt reasonably well, he was great: attentive, interested, and present. But that narrow window would close very quickly, and my brother and I were left with the longing for its re-opening. That wait sometimes lasted months. In the final stages of his life, when the mental illness had progressively diminished him and the Parkinson's took over his body, he seemed to lose his will to live. The undeniable truth in those last five to ten years was that the window was never going to open again. Fleeting glimpses of his old self, but nothing sustainable. That recognition was tough. Something that my brother and I fought. My father was there, but in most ways, not.

And then he fell into a coma.

I think I had lived long enough in that state of lack that I was ready to let him go. My brother was a different story. It was clear early on in the process that all of our father's brain functions had ceased and would never come back, yet my brother couldn't let go. It was hard watching my dad lying there month after month with no hope of his returning. And if he did return, what shape would he be in? The doctors emphasized that he would be a vegetable, but still, my brother was unwavering.

I got the best of Carl's parenting in my early years before his precipitous mental decline. My brother, who arrived five years after me, did not. By the time my brother was seven, our dad was a shell of his former self. I imagine that Andrew's longing wound was even more acute than mine. I think he was still unconsciously clinging to the idea that our dad would return and give him what he never received. Was he able to get any of that or process any of that in those nine months? He has never said, nor have we talked about it, but he clearly needed the time. It took him those nine months to finally let go. Although it was painful and frustrating for me to watch, I am grateful that I waited for him.

Then there were the extraordinary days of his death. Unusual to place extraordinary and death in the same sentence. And here are a few others: mysterious, magical, profound, supernatural. After my brother came around, papers were signed, and the date was set to remove my father from the machine that was breathing for him. I and Lena, my brother and his girlfriend, and my cousin Alan, one of our best friends, gathered in my dad's hospital room. It was morning. The nurses and doctors removed him from his breathing support. It was like watching Carl be born, taking his first independent breath in nine months. It was incredibly moving knowing that these breaths would be among his last. Parkinson's had taken his ability to irrigate his lungs so effectively we were going to watch him slowly drown.

All the rumors about a body preserving its own life till the last are completely true. By the end of day one, though his breath had become shallower, and we were informed that the liquid was slowly filling up his lungs, he was still very much alive and seemed not to be suffering. My brother and I both slept in the room with him on reclining chairs. The others returned to the hotel rooms. We woke up the next morning to coffee and donuts and a very alive father. How long could this take? No one could answer that question definitively. Two days? Three? A week? The vigil continued into the late afternoon, and my cousin went out to get us all sushi. Upon his return, we all gathered in a nearby lounge to dine on our spicy tuna rolls, yellowtail, and

Aga Tofu. Fifteen minutes into dinner, a nurse rushed out to inform us that my dad's pulse had dropped to a dangerously low level, and it appeared he was dying. We all rushed down the hall and into his room. The first thing I noticed was the light in the room. It was this radiant, soft, orange-yellow I had never seen before or since, like light at summer dusk but with an iridescent quality. Buddhist texts, Mala beads, and prayer books emerged. Tears began. And then my dad's pulse started to restore. Within ten minutes, it was back to normal. The light returned to its normal dull hospital opacity. What the hell had just happened? We were all confounded.

Later that evening, in our post-sushi, post near-death haze, a nurse came in, a nurse I had never consciously logged before. She asked if I would talk to her outside in the hallway. I followed her out.

 "Are you here to help your father die?" she

asked. "Of course," I replied.

"Well, in that case, you and the rest will have to leave." Dumbfounded silence laced with a touch of irritation.

She continued, "I have seen this before. Your dad is having too good of a time. He doesn't want to leave, and he won't."

"What are you asking me to do?"

"You all need to go back to the hotel. Don't spend the night here again."

Coma and consciousness. I had read books during the nine-month journey about folks in comas being present and aware on a subtle level. Visiting him throughout that nine-month process,

I was quite skeptical about these claims, yet I still talked to him, held his hand, and stroked his forehead. In that conversation the nurse was boldly confirming these claims. Except it was no longer theory, we had watched the truth of this unfold in real time. Maybe my dad had gotten something out of the nine-month process after all. No one will ever know for sure.

We left one at a time. I was the last to go. And was the last to see my father alive. We got the call at two am that he had passed.

On the ride from the hospital back home, Lena said, "It was like riding on the back of an enormous whale." I understood immediately what she meant. No control. Just submission to this massive, powerful, inexplicable process. The awe, the mystery of that process, is indelible. Nobody can tell me what I witnessed was hoo-hah. It was as real as it gets. And Lena, a person who was on the fence at the time about childrearing, said, "I have witnessed death, now I have to give birth." I didn't acknowledge it at the time, but that process sowed the seeds for my ultimate decision to become a dad later on. After Lena and I separated two years later, she became a momma.

It took me years to fully mourn his passing. There was also a huge relief. Watching him suffer was not easy. Watching him refuse to follow the doctor's orders to get better was not easy. Watching him fall further and further out of his day-to-day functioning and finally out of consciousness was excruciating, as was the care of him that was thrust on me in the final five years of his life. Death mercifully relinquished that obligation.

And there was something about his not being around that eased the constant reminder of the gene pool I emerged from. Maybe this would be the end of all of that mental struggle for all of us.

Wishful thinking. Taking the focus off of him placed it squarely back on myself.

There is a scene in Mama Mia II (I have watched a staggering number of "family movies" with my twelve-year-old daughter) at the very end of the film when Amanda Seyfried is walking down the aisle of the most charming hilltop Greek Island church that would move the most stalwart nonbeliever to worship. She is singing some ABBA song and holding her newborn baby, approaching the altar for baptism, when the specter of her deceased mother, played by Meryl Streep, appears and joins her in song. I lost it. My daughter had never seen me cry so hard. The moment became mine, facing the fact that my beloved deceased father would never meet his granddaughter. Carl would have adored her.

There was a dramatic moment, in the wind-down of his life in the assisted living facility, which changed everything for me. The facility wasn't far from where my brother lived at the time, in Westbury, Long Island. My brother would visit regularly. I learned later that Andrew was conducting very moving interviews with Carl that my brother recorded. There was one where Dad recited the Rudyard Kipling poem *IF*, his favorite poem, to Andrew, "…If you can fill the unforgiving minute/with sixty seconds' worth of distance run/Yours is the Earth and everything that's in it,/And-which is more-you'll be a Man, my son!" We played the entire recorded recitation at his funeral. It was so powerful hearing our dad's voice at his own funeral. My brother had the poem printed and laminated. It resides in my home to this day.

After his success at Burke Rehabilitation and subsequent collapse, I moved him into the assisted living facility. In the weeks after his admission, I would call the front desk looking to be patched through to his room. Connecting with him got progressively harder. The phone would ring through, and then I would get reconnected with the front desk.

"Where is my father?"

"He's not in his room."

"Well, where is he?"

"Let me check, Mr. Meyer." On hold. A five or ten-minute search. She returns.

"We don't know."

"You don't know? Then please find out."

"We're an assisted living facility home, sir, not a nursing home. The residents can come and go as they choose."

"We pay you a lot of money. Can you please try to locate him? He has Parkinson's disease."

"We will try, sir."

Days later, the same thing, virtually the same conversation, but I was angrier, more insistent, and was promised an answer by the head nurse. That answer came the next day. My dad was walking, shuffling, every day to the nearby Friendly's a mile away. A mile is a nice healthy jaunt for the average walker, but for a man with seizing Parkinson's, it's like running a marathon. And Carl took this walk every day. Every day.

"What do you order, Dad?"

"A banana split with hot fudge. Three scoops of ice cream."

What could I do? I surrendered. I had spent my entire adolescence and young adult life attempting to help this man make healthier choices. He did not want healthy choices. He wanted pleasure. How could I blame him? His life had become so small. It had been smaller than most for many years, boxed into the habitable places in his brain. Now all he wanted was his daily banana fucking split. Who was I to deprive him of that? At least he was getting out every day.

I've inherited my dad's craving for oral satisfaction. Kissing and cunnilingus often do the trick, but there are still edible satisfactions that even those delicacies can't replace. And I have become a pre-diabetic just like him, from years of caving to those temptations. Now I ply myself with popcorn and very dark chocolate- what my daughter refers to as cardboard- and bowls of low-sugar cereal. I have had to acquire new edible pleasures to save my own life. And it has worked. I initially lost twenty pounds and still go up and down depending on my emotional state and the season, but I still look forward to my daily fix of cardboard. My equivalent of a banana split.

There was this day at the adult home, the aforementioned crisis day, where I completely lost my shit. Through my twenties and thirties and well into my forties, I was very well-versed in losing my shit. A release from all the fear and anxiety. An illusion of control and certainly no fun for those on the receiving end. Ask my ex-wife. There was never really any fault in my logic, but as my former therapist used to say, my "delivery system" needed work. Sadly, over the years of his decline and abandonment by his girlfriend, I had become the target of his resentment, disappointment, and outrage at life. Who else did he have to exhaust himself upon? But on this particular day, I had enough. Unlike mine, my dad's tirades were mainly irrational. On this particular day, with Lena in the room, he started lacing into me about stealing his money. I attempted a rational defense but you can never meet rationality with delusion. After all the ways I was showing up for him, this tipped me. I got up and threw a wooden chair across the room. It hit the wall, bounced off, unbroken. It had the desired effect. It immediately derailed his tirade. I turned to him, and he looked stunned, childlike. And to further emphasize my point, I got up into his face.

"If you ever speak that way to me again, you won't see me anymore. Is that what you want?" He silently shook his head no.

"Do you hear me?" I said. He nodded.

"Do you understand?"

"Yes," he said.
I got up from his bedside chair and left the room and left the facility. On my way out, a neighboring room visitor who heard the ruckus said to me,

"How dare you treat your father that way?"

"Go fuck yourself. Mind your own damn business."

Years and years of oppression, disappointment, and perceived under-appreciation erupting in that moment. He had been declawed, defanged. I was finally able to come back at him without the fear of his reciprocity. Now, this may seem cruel, attacking an indefensible man, but for me, it became the pivot point of my independence.

****

After years of ever-progressive difficulty, failing couple's therapy, and her long trip to the Dakotas, my wife sprung the news on me that she wanted a "trial separation." She announced that she was in love with someone else. For my daughter's sake, we decided to cohabitate. I was in shock. Despite all the problems, I was still in love with Lois. I was hoping this new relationship would pass, but it didn't. Late-night whispered phone calls, staying out late. Classic shit. I was an alien in my own home. I slept on the couch or in my writing studio on the other side of the boarding school campus we lived on (she's still a teacher there) and visited my mother on weekends with Olivia to escape. Once the shock wore off, the grief and anxiety kicked in, followed closely by a deep and sustained depression that lasted months. I was paralyzed. All the symptoms I have outlined follows. It was hell. I am not sure how I parented successfully or how I got myself to work, it is all a blur.

I finally started pulling out of it and found a place to move to. I told her I was leaving after she returned from a Thanksgiving week with her new boyfriend. Two weeks later, I was out. It was a terrifying time, but somehow, I held it together thanks to the medication and my ability, learned from my father, to rebound and persevere. Going grocery shopping for the first time after moving, I dissolved into tears right in the middle of ShopRite.

We agreed upon joint custody of our daughter, and Olivia's joining me in my new, very temporary place felt like an adventure for us both. She really liked it there, and eventually, so did I. It was in New Paltz, a college town and tourist destination twenty-five minutes from our former family home. It's a walking town with a movie theatre, an independent bookstore, and many great places to eat and shop. We spent many a day exploring the town on foot. All the activity in the town helped us both.

The day we had laid the news on Olivia about the separation was one of the hardest of my life, and likely hers too. Initially, she seemed to take it fine, but then she broke down. Her worry- having heard about this from other friends of divorce- was that she would only see me on weekends. She crept into my arms, and I reassured her that her mom and I would be sharing the time with her every week and that she would see me a lot. That fact settled her down. The entire scene was heartbreaking. On the days she was with me, there was a lot to focus on taking care of her and having fun together. When she went back with her mother, I was faced with my aloneness and the rest of my life. It was daunting. The leading sign that "the ground had risen" (a term used by my doctor to describe the process of coming out of depression- when depressed, it was like the bottom had dropped out) was when it started to become more difficult to sleep. The body no longer needed as much antidepressant, so the extra would start to overrev the system. Every time this happened, my dose was lowered, and before long, my sleep would return to something that resembled normal. This time, however, I still couldn't settle down, even when I was taken off the medicine completely. My doctor asked me to come in.

****

I thought that all the extra stress and anxiety brought upon by the separation might be the cause. The doctor, who had been watching my process for some time, now concluded that what I was experiencing was referred to as hypomania. She described that even without the antidepressant, I was still revving high and couldn't come down. Imagine being adrenalized at the gym, playing any sport, dancing at a club, and that feeling which feels so good at the time, won't stop. This, she explained, was causing this recent bout of sleep deprivation. We all know the feeling.

Staring at the ceiling in the middle of the night, trying anything. Pacing, counting the cracks in the ceiling. Nothing would help. At some point, I would nod off, but it was never enough. I walked around revved up and also exhausted. Hypomania is the flip side of depression. Better than hypermania, which is what my father had, but clearly, still quite difficult. Another indicator was that my depressive episodes were becoming more prolonged. She prescribed me a second drug, Lamictal, a mood stabilizer. When I was on the train going home, I googled hypomania. What came up immediately was Bipolar II. I was in shock. Did I always have what my father had? Was this what I was running from my entire life? Long periods of depression, longer than Bipolar I, and manic episodes that were much less severe than BP I- No hallucinations, no feeling like the king of the world, no late-night drives, no spending sprees, most of which my dad had experienced. Over-revved hypomania caused bouts of irritability and snappy anger. A short fuse, as they say. And, of course, the sleep deprivation. I recognized all of these symptoms. I had had them for years. But…. the hypo side also felt really good. I had never suspected a problem when I was in this mode because I had tons of energy and was incredibly creative and productive.

I had come out of this episode disoriented- no marriage, living in a place that was hip and beautiful, but where I was starting over and knew no one. The break with my wife had coincided with my stepping down as the artistic director of the theatre I had co- founded. The intent of that decision was to lighten my load so I could slow down. What was there to throw myself into to distract me from the enormous feelings? Additionally, I had to find more teaching work to afford my new life and also learn how to become a part-time single parent. I was completely disoriented.

****

This is from The Mayo Clinic on the differences between Bipolar I and II:

"Mania is more severe than hypomania. It causes more noticeable problems at work, school and social activities, as well as getting along with others. Mania also may cause a break from reality, known as psychosis. You may need to stay in a hospital for treatment.

Hypomanic episodes include three or more of these symptoms:

- Being much more active, energetic, or agitated than usual.

- Feeling a distorted sense of well-being or too self-confident.

- Needing much less sleep than usual.
- Being unusually talkative and talking fast.

- Having racing thoughts or jumping quickly from one topic to another."

After feeling good, there is always a high risk that a depressive episode will follow. "The crash." Looking back on it these symptoms started to become more acute in my mid 20's. But I never really paid it any mind because this was how I always was when I wasn't depressed. This was what 'not-depressed' felt like. Tons of energy felt awesome coming out of a period where it was near impossible to drag myself out of bed.

But… to learn that this is the flip side of being Bipolar and not just "who I am' was staggering to realize. To see the inner workings of your life laid out in print as an illness was shocking, painful, and daunting. My past had finally caught me at the age of fifty-seven.

And then there are the side effects from the various drugs to be careful of. The first antidepressant drug I took while still married, Paxil, gave me a dry mouth and made it almost impossible to have an orgasm. Moving to Celexa completely eliminated both of those symptoms. The Lamictal, the mood stabilizer prescribed for bipolar issues, seems to carry no apparent side effects. The one remaining effect I have wrestled with, exacerbated by the antidepressant, is weight gain. Food has been an issue for all the men in my nuclear family. We have all taken antidepressants, which definitely exacerbates the issue. All my dad, brother, and I had to do was look at yummy, high-caloric food, and we'd gain weight. It seems that my brother has mainly thrown up his arms in defeat and eats what he wants. He carries an unhealthy amount of weight. My dad lived for many years and went into a coma before he died, obese. I continue to wrestle with this despite my dependency on these drugs. During some periods I feel in complete control of what I eat, counting both calories and steps. Other times, I struggle. Food can feel so comforting, but when I get on the scale after a period of excess, I feel like crap. I always feel great when I am lighter and leaner. So why can't I break that compulsion once and for all? I see people eat anything they want and gain no weight. My stepdad was one of those types. It's baffling to me. Delicious food is so pleasurable. Being in a relationship helps. I can get my oral satisfaction in even more pleasurable ways. My doctor tells me, "You have to feel hungry at the end of every meal."

Fuck that. That is not how I will live the rest of my life. Hungry. Moderation is my goal. Sticking to a certain number of calories or in a specific range, occasionally giving myself a diet vacation.

Prayer on this helps me. Praying for intercession is a big part of the twelve-step programs. It works for many. It works for me… when I use it. Am I a food addict? Maybe. I definitely have the propensity some days toward binging, but I can usually stop myself. I am currently five to ten pounds heavier than I'd like to be, which isn't a ton. But getting down to my desired weight is hard. My daughter tries to keep me on track, "Your belly is bigger, Dad," she told me last night. "I know, honey," I replied. "It's hard."

In the 1960's, when I was a child, sugar was king. The scientific community had not yet caught on to the damaging effect they now know sugar has on our health. The cereal manufacturers took advantage of this by advertising their miracle breakfasts as "Fortified with vitamins and minerals." My mother and most of the ones I knew, bought this completely. That they were doing the right thing by us kids sending us to school all "fortified."

They had no idea that they were feeding us poison. I woke up every morning and had a wide variety of sugar-laden cereals stored on top of the fridge- Captain Crunch, Fruit Loops, Apple Jacks, Lucky Charms, Frosted Flakes, and Count Chocula among many others on rotation. What amazes me is that these brands still dominate the cereal aisles of most major supermarkets. Sure, there are many more healthy alternatives to choose from, but every time we pass these boxes, my daughter clambers for them. I guide her into less sugary choices occasionally acquiescing for a one serving size snack. Growing up consuming bowls of sugar on a daily basis turned me into a sugar addict, like many others in this country. Combine this with normal sugary dessert items and the cans of sugared soda at the park playing sports, and I was far gone by the time I turned twelve. I have greatly reduced my intake, but I still need my sugar "methadone" to satisfy that craving. Nonsugar candy and chewing gum (laden with poison sugar substitutes) and a healthier choice- fruit. I have replaced the soda with Stevia-based soda, which has its own chemical processing issues but is certainly healthier, and once in a while, I indulge in Diet Coke or Doctor Pepper, which I know possesses the same sugar substitute poison. I rationalize that a little poison won't kill me. Silly, I know. But the taste of those beverages has been nearly impossible to let go of.

****

Many folks who suffer from Bipolar I or II end up, at some point in their lives, in a mental institution. As of yet, thank God, that hasn't been my fate. I have thought about it and asked my psychiatrist if a stay would help during the post-marriage episode, but she didn't recommend it. I was able to get through the darkest moments of that episode with the aid of increased medicine dosages, more weekly sessions of therapy, and all my psychological and spiritual tools. The depression that I normally experienced seemed to last several months, but this episode persisted endlessly. After the fourth month, I came close to checking myself into the hospital for the first time in my life. Reminding me what it was like in those places, traumatically experienced on too many visits to my dad as a young lad, is what finally kept me from following through. My psychiatrist thought it could do more harm than good being surrounded by all of that, reactivating the feelings that being a visitor all those many years ago evoked, this time being the one inside. I am sure she was right. The only possible development that could thrust me in there would be suicidal ideations getting to a point where I was actually planning action. Gratefully, that moment has not arrived.

It took me at least a year to get over the impact of the news of my new Bipolar II diagnosis. Finally, after years of internal running and some literal running away behavior as well (sexing, overeating, overworking), I was forced by my own disease to face the reality that I was more like my father in this capacity than I was ever able to admit. There were years when I rejected my father and didn't visit for long stretches at a time, and his illness was too frightening for me to face. Even in the facility I placed him in before he died, I should have visited him more. His behavior and his mental and emotional state were too disturbing for me to experience. This is a guilt I will live with until I take my last breath. Fortunately, in the days leading up to the coma he would never return from, we were able to express our deep love for each other. I am grateful, but this still provides cold comfort for my inattentiveness during those months. I know I had done a ton for him throughout his life and especially in his final years- managing several mental facility stays, adult care, home aids, Burke Rehab for his Parkinson's disease- and I was protecting my thirty-four-year-old self. But the guilt still persists.

On the other hand, as a person on the self-consciousness path I knew that awareness was the key to recovery. Still, it was excruciatingly hard news. Every morning and evening, when I take the pills that stave off the effects of this disorder, I am reminded of the illness I possess. It remains humbling and frightening. But I take the medicine religiously.

It was hard to admit to myself, and then to the women I was on the cusp of relationships with, that I had Major Depressive Disorder. To admit that I had Bipolar disorder felt like a life sentence of aloneness unless I found someone who also suffered from this same illness as my dad did in the latter stages of his life. Although met with some concern and many questions it has not, as yet, sent anyone packing. In fact, the ones who really care about me and see me seem to see past the malady and trust in my commitment to my daily medicinal regimen. However, whenever there is a new potential paramour, I am still filled with anxiety in the anticipation of the impending talk.

****

Escape. That modality has been embedded in my behavior. Not wanting to occupy the space that has been allotted to me, not wanting to feel the feelings. Not wanting to be anywhere near there. Where do I want to be? I am never really sure, but just not in that space. What is in that space? A restlessness, a deep fear that something is coming to get me. I feel a tightness in my midriff, anticipating the downward spiral, and in the up times, a lingering fear that the ground will give way soon.

What helps me stay in the moment? Same as the antidotes for relief from my illness. Alanon meetings for sure, therapy sessions (though there is at times still a resistance to confront certain issues), music, the right natural surroundings (I have experienced bliss in there), meditation (though my mind can still behave like a bucking bronco), sport (there is nowhere else you can be but in the moment, every moment competing) and connection with the right trusted human. Revealing my fears and unsettledness can go a long way in settling me down. In Alanon, there are two pertinent slogans: "You're as sick as your secrets" and "Sharing your issues, fears, and secrets makes them half as potent." Sometimes these practices aid me in actually joining the moment or at least get me a lot closer to it. The inner observer, often frightened, quiets down. That is a form of serenity that all of us on the spiritual/healing path seek- a release from worries

143

and fears. Certain phases in relationships can also ground me. Things are tranquil; there isn't imminent work to do. When we are discovering each other, there is this pure mutual appreciation and fascination. So tender, so thrilling.

Another important contributor to my inner sense of peace: is when the focus is not on me. This happens when my focus is on my students, my daughter, writing, and aiding someone in Alanon. All these require a constancy of focus. The danger is putting too much focus on the other and losing myself. I want a guarantee of love right away, which I know is impossible. But that's the irrational product of my childhood. I think one of the reasons I want to run right to love is to guarantee certainty. To live in doubt, in the possibility of estrangement, alienation feels too crushing, the possibility of vacancy too barren. At the slightest signs of disapproval, my instinct is to flee.

I am learning how to work with the discomfort. It doesn't mean I don't want to flee; it's bringing a commitment to not fleeing. I work my entire tool kit to not run or blow up a bridge. Staying in the present, sitting in the momentary potential of disappointment, rejection, and alienation, can feel completely untenable, but I am learning to do it.

I have also learned how to disagree and confront in a healthier way. Initially, it was sloppy and harsh because it was so unbearably scary and also a product of what Lena called "building a bomb." Stuffing the desire to say "No," "That hurt," or "Please don't do that." After a while, all those small hurts build-up, and one innocuous catalyst can generate rage. Later, I learned how to confront sooner with less attack and later still with a degree of growing trust that the response wouldn't result in rejection, outcasting, or obliteration. That's how it felt so often in my childhood home, rendering objection dangerous and eventually impossible.

I have found that a healthy understanding of what is unacceptable behavior, followed by a discussion with as little blame as possible, can create an even healthier relationship. It also keeps me out of my head, dwelling in fears of the unknown outcome of speaking up.

****

As many relationships did during COVID-19, mine with Hannah, the new relationship, turned complicated. We both had a child and in that unknown period when the CDC and Fauci were still figuring out what the hell this plague was, we were both on lockdown, as much of the country was. Zoom sessions began with the world and between the two of us and even occasional Zoom sex, novel at first but a far cry from the real thing. Better than nothing, we rationalized. After masking began and more research revealed how the virus was transmitted, I floated the idea that we start seeing each other. Creating a pod of sorts. She was evasive initially and then told me she wasn't comfortable being in person. Even though we were both on Zoom, me teaching and she with her clients, there was still out-in-the-world interaction, as my daughter had returned to in-person learning which made her uncomfortable; despite the mandatory masking, this still made Hannah uncomfortable.

Were these legitimate fears, or was it a seemingly valid reason masking her deeper concern about my mental-emotional state? I chose not to ask.

I could cajole a few in person meetings, but only outdoors and positively no kissing. This became unbearable. Even when we became boosted with the first shots, she was still reticent to resume. The same rules would apply. Not long after, we both knew that this was untenable and decided to take a break.

We remained in touch, but the contact was sporadic and painful.

Despite the difficulty and frustration, how could I fault her for wanting to protect herself and her child? I also had a child to protect, but since Olivia had returned to school in person and I was back in the classroom teaching acting, there was no ready solution. Hannah's child was still at home doing online classes, and she was still conducting her client sessions online. Our future together hung in the balance.

****

From a young age, I knew I wanted to be a father. At some point, I lost contact with that need. Likely it eroded slowly over time, dealing with the impact of my family's damage. Just like my esophageal passage closing off, so went the way of my gifts and passions. The epic failure of years spent trying to make my father right shattered my self-esteem. Everything I did back then was in dialogue with my father's condition, either implicitly or explicitly. I learned much later that these behaviors and feelings are prototypical for the family orbiting around a diseased member, whether a disability, mental illness, or addiction. One's own needs become buried. They have not yet discovered drugs that manage this obsession. Programs like Alanon, Co-Dependents Anonymous, and weeklong family retreats at places like the Caron Foundation were the only antidotes available. Therapy helped, but without those programs, I don't think I would have made much progress. Therapy hadn't significantly improved those behaviors before I discovered those other paths. Years of practice, and I mean years, decades, taught me how to

146

accept my father's disease and the alcoholism of my stepfather and stepbrothers, and slowly, progressively lay down the job of fixing.

And in the midst of that letting go, I rediscovered that ebullient, talented boy who I had been and the man I was becoming. Buried the deepest was the long-repressed need to be a father.

Lena and I broke up in part because she was nearing the end of her baby conceiving window, and I just wasn't ready. There were many other reasons, but this one was the most imminent and most pressing. I was thirty-seven at the time. Lena was two years older than me, approaching forty very rapidly. My soon-to-be wife, Lois, was conveniently twelve years my junior, permitting me to kick the baby-making can way down the road, or so I thought.

Six months after we met, Lois announced her strong need to have a chile. I bobbed and weaved for nine years, forestalling the decision. I legitimately wasn't ready. Lois was. After nine years, she thirty-four, me, forty-six the moment of truth arrived. She took a sabbatical from her teaching job and went to the East for a year, pursuing her Buddhist passions. If, at the end of that year my decision hadn't changed, she would need to move on. That year was excruciating. Despite the agreement that we could see other people, which provided some necessary distraction, that choice hung like a guillotine high above my neck.

Up until this point I had two reasons that having a child would be too great a risk for me. The first had to do with my career. I had worked so tirelessly to attain a modest living in the theatre that I imagined that a family life with a child would jeopardize that. That I would suddenly have to work at Starbucks, or worse, put a suit back on and abandon my passion altogether. During the search for my calling, through my thirtieth birthday, I worked a series of soul-sucking jobs, including the job that sustained me during the years I was studying acting- working for my dear cousin Alan and his cosmetic accessory and fragrance businesses. There were points when the day-to-day grind of this life moved me deep into a long depression and many thoughts of taking my own life. It wasn't until I finally left his employ and started my acting teaching business that that work-related suffering abated. In retrospect, those experiences gave me an advantage as an artist: I had advanced skills in the necessary business pursuit in the field, which, sadly, many gifted artists don't possess. They are often forced out of their chosen profession and into compromised work, practicing their craft on the fringes of their lives.

The second was my abject fear of family and my inability to father properly. By then, I knew that I had Major Depressive Disorder, and I had witnessed and experienced the effects of living around a diseased patriarch. I did not want to visit that on anyone. What would I have done if I had known back then about my Bipolar diagnosis? I think that it would likely have prevented me from going forward. Why do we learn things about ourselves when we do? The spiritual perspective is that "God gives us only what we can handle." There were three forces that intervened on behalf of taking the leap.

The first, as odd as it may sound, was the experience of watching our adopted cat give birth to her litter. Lois, a devoted cat person, had been without one for about a year after losing two to what they call "Cat Aids," an incurable virus. We were then living in an apple orchard, and periodically, cat owners would dump their animals on the farm. It was later explained that cat owners, rationalizing their decision, believed that their animals would be well cared for by farm types. That was true to an extent. All the residents on the farm - there were twelve of us, plus workers - would feed them in a barn on the property adjacent to the converted barn we lived in. These cats would, over time, become wild and distrustful of humans. A return of sorts to their true natures. They would never approach when we fed them. The following day we would return to empty bowls. Most of these cats would eventually disappear, likely having assumed their place on the food chain.

One day a Siamese appeared on the farm, and my ex fell in love. At first, we thought that such a beautiful cat had lost her way. We put up signs in the neighborhood and called the local shelters to see if anyone had inquired. No one responded. Within that week, Lois fell out of love, and Uli became my cat. She had clearly been abused and initially was terrified of touch. Perhaps she recognized in me a compassion and empathy for abuse. In any case, we quickly bonded.

We soon discovered why Uli - after the verb ululate, a sound made as an expression of strong emotion- was dumped on the farm. At our first vet visit, it was revealed that she was pregnant. They estimated her age at three or four. Since cats can have litters from six months old we could only imagine how many litters she had already had. We speculated that initially, she was bred with other Siamese cats, but over time she must have gotten out and been impregnated by other non-Siamese toms. This was apparent when her litter arrived.

This is the advice we received about preparing for the arrival of these kittens: Find a box high enough to keep the babies in and low enough for momma to get in and out for food and water. Then, find a warm and private dark space for the delivery, put the box there, and keep showing momma the spot. On the day of the kittens' arrival, my ex was away on a Buddhist retreat so it was just me and Uli, which felt fitting. When it became clear she was starting labor, I brought her into the box in the closet. She jumped out and got into bed with me. I took her back into the box again. Again she found her way back into bed. This went on several more times until I finally acquiesced. She proceeded to have her babies lying next to me in bed. The kittens were born on my left thigh.

It was a magical, powerful experience. I had never witnessed labor before. This was the closest one could get to midwifing cat labor. A kitten would come; she would lick off the translucent sac that encased them, clean them, and help them find a nipple. Then she would rest. Twenty or so minutes later, the next delivery began. She had four kittens. At the very end, when I brought her babies into the box, she attempted to bring them back into my bed. This time, after one or two more rounds of transport, she acquiesced and settled into her blanketed box in the closet, just a few paces away from her food and water.

I was blown away. There was a twinge of a hint of a crack about having my own child that opened up inside of me that evening.

The second nudge to my resistance occurred on the aforementioned trip to India to see my sponsored child Nagalakshmi. I think the endurance of that relationship over ten years and the mutual devotion I experienced on that visit revealed what intimacy between a father and child could feel like. Being surrounded by Naga, who never left my side, and the community of young beaming faces following me around the village had an indelible impact. Added to all of this was the overriding purpose of the trip east: to see where Lois and I stood post-separation. I was en route to Nepal, where Lois was. The visit to Naga's village was a stopover on the way, and what hung in the balance in Nepal was the question of whether we would have a child together.

This leads to the last and perhaps most overwhelming factor. After my time with Lois in Nepal, I realized that I loved her too much to let her go. I had already left a cherished relationship with Lena with the same childbearing issue, having heavily influenced our decision to split. The last thing I wanted to do was leave this relationship for the same reason. There was no more can to kick or road left to kick it down. The love I felt for Lois tipped the scales. After she returned from the East and it was clear that we both still wanted a future together, I made my decision. I would marry this woman, and we would try to have a child.

My daughter Olivia arrived on October 5, 2012, just after I had turned fifty. I was certainly not the first fifty-year-old to enter fatherhood, but we quinquagenarian fathers are still outliers. They say fatherhood is a young man's game, and those first two years certainly tested that theory. I can say without reservation that her arrival altered my life for the better in every way. I had overcome hardships and challenges and was wiser for it. I felt ready.

Agreeing to try to have a child was the rightest thing I ever did. I was going to say decision but no amount of inner debate could have led to an actual choice. I needed that visit to Nepal and triage of support to get to that place: therapist, healer, and psychiatrist. All loving master practitioners and guides. I owe them everything. They would say that I showed up and did the work. That may be true, but without their skillful handling, the clarity to get where I had arrived would certainly have eluded me.

****

What is "the work" as it relates to any healing phase? Showing up is a huge part, even when I don't want to. I work on being present, not running away, and learning how to accept whatever comes up. Study and writing are a part of it – spiritual reading, psychological reading (Alice Miller's <u>Drama of the Gifted Child</u> is a hugely impactful read), Alanon literature, and Alanon workbooks. Being honest with the people in the Alanon meetings, in retreat, and with therapists, doctors, and psychiatrists. I am forever amazed by what certain friends I know don't tell their therapists. Why not tell them everything once you have built up trust? If one can't work on the pivotal issues with a therapist, where can you work on them? Alanon has a slogan- "You're as sick as your secrets." Wisdom. Those secrets affect and also distort my seeing, thinking, and behaving. I have also coined a credo: "You can't work on your mind with your mind." My experience suggests that there are issues that our minds are protecting us from and put up an excellent reasoned defense of why we are OK and don't need assistance or, for that matter, to change at all, which is why it takes many people a full-on collapse to finally seek help. I have certainly had those collapses and will do anything to avoid another one.

I am a good student. Tell me what to do to feel better, and I will do it. The tasks I have before me usually have to do with facing my trauma and my fears, and taking action even when my confidence is waning. I build confidence, and courage by taking action. Humility. That's another important part of the work. Being a know-it-all cuts me off from learning, from changing. I want to be teachable. Lastly, I am motivated by my desire to enjoy life. There were pockets of happiness, even delight, as a kid. That feeling became a touchstone throughout my recovery. I wanted to get back to that.

Speaking of delight, the past eleven years being Olivia's dad has filled me with buckets of it. I adore her. She is sleeping right in front of me as I write this. Even as she turns eleven years old, I can still just sit and watch her sleep in complete devotion. I never imagined loving anyone so completely and fully. I was hooked from the moment the doctor asked me to cut the umbilical cord between Olivia and her mother, which is something I never would have done under normal circumstances. Remember, me and medical school and blood. The umbilicus, the entire thing, is a miracle. I feel so lucky to have been in the room and a part of that experience. I don't see how any adult who hasn't had a child can ever really understand that awe.

Lois' delivery was hard. I have heard of harder ones, but forty one hours rates. We had every intention of proceeding naturally. We went through all the classes, chose a hospital that had a natural birthing wing and worked with a lovely midwife, but when push came to shove- pun intended- the doctor had to be called in to deliver the goods. At the twenty-seventh hour, my wife attempted to reduce her suffering in their calming Jacuzzi. She had invited me in with her, and after I sat down, our thighs grazed.

"Don't Touch Me!" she

yelled. "What?"

"Just don't fucking touch me!"

I knew she could yell, but this had reached an entirely different pitch. And then, with a deranged look in her eye,

"This is all a nice idea, but I need pain medication. I need it NOW!"

Who was I, or anyone, to reason her out of it? Seven epidurals. Seven. As soon as they administered the medicie into her spine she was restored to her relaxed self. You could see, as the medicine would start to wear off, that deranged look begin to return. At about the fortieth hour, after the last epidural, Lois started to spike a fever. That is when the game changed. A fever stresses the baby and raises her heart rate. In came the doctor and a suction device that fit on the crown of the head to help pull the baby out.

"If we don't get your baby out of you," the doctor said, "we are going to have to open you up to get her."

After forty-one hours, many of those hours suffering, it felt like a crime to have Lois go under the knife. I leaned into her ear,

"You didn't come this far to be cut open!"

And like some coach on steroids I leaned in and started attempting to encourage her. The delivery process began. The heaving, the strained face, the screams. All the things we are familiar with from the movies. But unlike those dramas, we were now playing beat the clock. There was some kind of time limit, I think fifteen minutes before we reached the Cesarean cut-off. And with the help of the head suction, Lois pushed out our miracle.

It was revealed very quickly that the baby had the same fever her mom had. Sharing blood, how could she not? After the moment she took her first breath, and Lois had her obligatory first snuggle, Olivia was instantly whisked from us to the Neonatal Intensive Care Unit. I followed, of course, and in distress, watched as they tried to find a vein in our darling's arm or leg or anywhere. I am the guy who looks away when the needles go in for my annual blood test. This was torture, more so that this was how my kid was spending her first moments on the planet. They finally found a vein. Olivia never cried, not once during that vein-finding process, not once when the needle went in. A portend of things to come. Starting at five, Olivia wanted to be there when her grandfather tested his blood sugar levels and injected himself with insulin. She is fearless, unlike her wimpy father. So there she was, lying on a gurney with the antibiotic dripping in to treat the fever. I tentatively sidled up to her gurney and said her name. Then another miracle. Almost instantly, she turned her head towards me, reached out her tiny hand, and touched my face. I was overwhelmed. I had an immediate sense that we had known each other forever and were saying hello again. "Hello dear one, great to see you again."

I was one of those husbands who would talk to the baby in her momma's stomach. Could she have recognized my voice? I do talk loudly, and resonantly, and I did a lot of belly touching during the pregnancy. Needless to say, I was hers forever. And in that instance, something else blossomed in me. There was a dormant secret chamber of my heart that had opened, and it has never closed. It seems to open incrementally wider every day.

The other aspect of fatherhood that I quickly felt was a need to protect. I have never protected anybody or anything so fiercely in my entire life. I have been devoted to a lot of things, my writing life, my teaching, and my marriage, but this was devotion on an entirely other plane. This baby was my master teacher of devotion.

And I have Lois to thank for all of this. In the first year as a couple, she was twenty-six, me thirty-eight, and she started banging the drum for a baby. I was so far from ready. I will always be grateful to her for her unwavering need to have a baby and for making that need known, loudly, and continuously. And reminding me that I would be a great father. And also making it very clear that if I maintained my "No" she would need to find someone who would be a "Yes."

Olivia and I are so much alike in so many ways, and this can lead to some head-butting. But that is more than eclipsed by all the fun love, and laughs we share. She is willful, very funny, super smart, athletic, and empathetic beyond her years. Her teachers and other adults have noted this. I recognize myself in her. We attended a Tibetan Buddhist teaching in the latter stage of Lois' pregnancy. At the very end of the teaching, it is customary for the Rimpoche to exit down the main aisle of the hall through his audience of practitioners while everyone stands. On this day, he approached us and stopped, looked at me, then Lois' pregnant belly and then back to me.

"Looks like you," he said, and then the procession continued down the aisle and out of the hall.

I am not sure that Olivia does look like me. I look at photographs of my younger self and I do see the resemblance. Most people think she most closely resembles her mother. The likeness we share is characterological. Is that what the Rimpoche meant?

My daughter was born with colic, an incredibly misunderstood condition. I was colic as a kid, which of course, I have no memory of, but I understand it was as difficult on my parents as it was on Lois and me. Wild outbreaks of screaming and tears from the baby, wakeful nights rocking, rocking, rocking our daughter to try and settle her down, one of us moving to the car's back seat to soothe her while the other drove. After weeks of this and more than our share of desperation, we were recommended to read a book called <u>The Happiest Baby on the Block</u> by Harvey Karp. Weird title, and life-saving information. This pediatrician had spent the better part of his career researching colic. Long misunderstood as caused by gastrointestinal discomfort, he laid out a theory and approach that made complete sense and was easy to follow. His strong opinion was that colic babies, who may very well have underdeveloped digestive systems, were not fully formed in three trimesters and were not yet ready from a developmental perspective to emerge from the womb into the world. That they needed a fourth trimester. But of course, that is not what Mother Nature would permit, and even if she could, the baby's head would be too large to pass through the uterus and out the vagina after twelve months inside. And I know my ex could not have handled three more months carrying Olivia.

The doctor's plan provides guidance in how parents can simulate a womblike experience to allow the baby to have her fourth trimester out in the world. This system included swaddling, a practice that had been accepted for years but somehow had fallen out of favor. It made sense that this tightly wrapped environment would simulate a womb. There were special rocking techniques that accompanied the swaddling. There was also a CD included with the book. This CD was a collection of sounds to help the baby relax. One would think that this collection of sounds would have been filled with the greatest hits of baby songs, nursery rhymes, birds chirping, and the sound of gentle rain falling. After the complete effectiveness of these sounds, my ex went on her computer and burned copies of this CD so we could keep it in both of our cars and near all of our stereo equipment. When she burned these CDs on iTunes, the sounds were classified as "heavy metal." You read that right. This magical elixir of sound included all measures of loud, intense, shocking noises: planes taking off, hairdryers running, washing machines churning, and my daughter's personal favorite: the continuous sounds of a vacuum cleaner. Counterintuitive as it may seem, we learned that the sound inside of a womb is cacophonous for a child- loud continuous heartbeat, blood running through veins and arteries, digestive fluid periodically breaking down the food in the stomach and small intestine. So these disruptive sounds to an adult ear were soothing to a baby's. Amazing. To say this worked like a charm is an understatement. Literally, seconds, after we cued up the CD, the crying and screaming, would abruptly stop, and calm would reign. This was a lifesaver for all of us.

One day while we were driving together, Olivia kicked into her predictable wailing. I immediately reached to turn on the CD, which was a permanent fixture in the car player. On this day, however, no sound emerged. I panicked, although not too intensely, lest I drive us into a ditch. I remembered the category that iTunes had specified: Heavy Metal. I pulled the car over and sifted through the glove compartment, looking for something that was heavy metal-esque, my days of Kiss and Aerosmith, which were barely heavy metal, had long since passed, and then I discovered Nirvana's "Nevermind." Would grunge suffice? I desperately tossed the CD into the player like a football quarterback throwing a Hail Mary pass into the end zone. Nirvana's classic "Smells like Teen Spirit" squealed out of the speakers. Instantly my daughter settled into quiet contentment and minutes later fell asleep. The Happiest Baby CD never reappeared in my car again. From that moment on it was Nirvana all the way. As she got older and could speak, Olivia would ask for Nirvana by name and start swaying and singing along to Teen Spirit. We have that on video. It is both hilarious and amazing to watch as she keeps a perfect beat swaying her body and hands and then joining in with "Hello, hello, hello." It is not what Kurt Cobain envisioned, but it is a wonderful effect of his music nonetheless.

Sometime later, reflecting on why so many of us were and are intoxicated by rock and roll, this story came to mind. This music, the heavy driving beat, and the loud yet harmonious sounds must bring us back to our womblike experience. This must be why, I surmised, rock and roll was a revelation for the world. Every culture has its version of this heavy driving beat, but many countries went crazy for the rock sound, just like my kid and me.

How does this all relate to mental illness? Well, in the Disney version, this cured the depression for good. Cure by baby. The extra chamber opened up in my heart, casting the beast back to wherever the beast came from. And that illusion was sustained for a time. But not permanently. I had two serious bouts of depression in the first six years of my daughter's life. And then a third right after Covid. I didn't like that average. Neither of the two bouts was her fault. Even with Olivia on the scene, my mind eventually moved to suicide. All that love and devotion did not ameliorate the agony, the hopeless despair. What her presence did do is keep me going, move me forward, and remain in the solution. She is always my most powerful mental health motivator. Even in those dark states, her presence gave me a modicum of joy. I reiterate this to remind myself when the depression descends again that I want to live. For me and for her. And for others. Before my mother's death, I couldn't see how that elderly woman would have survived me taking my life.

Some of my closest friends would be put at risk. One of the friends, in particular, suffers from mental issues and flirts with suicide as well. And all of my present and former students. All of the inspiration we have gleaned through the processes together. This, as the final answer just isn't sufficient. But for my daughter, most of all.

COVID-19 has been the only episode in the last five years. How I cared for my kid during that I have no clue. Perhaps that joy and the love we share got me up in the morning to take her to school. Since then, almost three and half years ago, there have been no incidences of depression, and though days I feel sped up and sometimes agitated, no prolonged manic episodes.

Covid was, for so many of us, the most trying time in our lives. Only a select few survivors remember the suffering and breadline of the great depression, and the impact of those who endured and perished, and still die from Aids is specific mainly to a segmented population. Covid was a once in a generation global disaster. One that many of us didn't know if we'd ever collectively recover from.

For me, I went right into crisis mode, which I have said, I am highly skilled in. I shifted all of my classes online, which miraculously was successful enough to keep my businesses alive. Zoom was the saving grace of COVID-19 for so many. But… the isolation…and the fact that several projects, ones that I had been working toward for years and were going into production, were canceled, and as it turned out, were never rescheduled again. For a bipolar with major depression issues, this was a nightmare. I needed to get all sorts of medicinal adjustments during this period and could have driven me to my first institutional stay, but as we all experienced, hospitals were the worst place to be during the crisis. I hung on for dear life. Taking care of my daughter so many days really helped, as did teaching online, though some days I dreaded it and pushed through. Acting training on Zoom. It seemed counterintuitive. But somehow, it worked.

Will this last?

That is the question I live with. I am grateful that it's not something I obsess about or even think about that much, but when the thought does arrive, it is a cause of anxiety. Amnesia is a wonderful thing. They say women who decide to have a second child don't remember with distinct clarity the physical agony they endured giving birth. And if there is recollection, it doesn't match the intensity of the actual experience. A species-sustaining mechanism. Mercifully, the same is true with the depths of depression. Once actively back in my robust life, the memory of the excruciating symptoms of depression faded. Even writing this now, the symptoms of darkness are more a distant memory, a residue of its impact. The prospect of a return exists, but the awareness of that probability diminishes with time especially as I get farther and farther away from the last episode.

"You are not your father." That refrain echoes during difficult times, amplified by years of reminders by therapists. Today I believe that, but it did take me a while. What lingers is Carl's response or non-response to his drugs. The way the doses were constantly being altered trying to fight the beast. They never fully succeeded. This is not my fate. Things are well. I have and am responding to the daily medication, but I do live with the question of the longitudinal effectiveness of these drugs. The longer I remain well, the more the science of pharmacology develops, which provides reassurance. My Alanon program teaches me to stay in the moment. Don't project into the future. "Don't trouble until trouble troubles you." Most days, I don't.

****

The arrival of my daughter accelerated the healing that had already begun between myself and my mom. I knew in my heart that my daughter and my mother needed a relationship with each other.

I made an unstated commitment to visit my mother once a month with Olivia, which was not as simple as that sounds. We lived two hours from her, and when we moved to Woodstock to be near her new school, two and a half. If you know anything about travel to Long Island, heading out at the wrong time can tack on thirty to sixty minutes to that trip. Traffic is the kiss of death for any Long Island commuter. I tried to make my trips at off-peak travel times, but it always seems like something on those highways creates delays even late at night. That's when the construction teams come out. As such, those visits inevitably became sleepovers. That's a lot of concentrated time with a woman I had so much complicated history with.

My mother's delight in being with my daughter was the elixir. She was thrilled to have a relationship with Olivia, and although much softened and grateful, she was still quite capable of being difficult. My daughter was learning impulse control, but, like most children, in the three to seven-year-old range didn't have much. Unfortunately, neither had my septuagenarian mother. And if willfulness is a genetic trait, my daughter inherited an abundance of it from my mom. When the two of them were in a peaceful place; watching them together was an absolute joy, the mutual love and appreciation so deep. But, when either or both of them got triggered, all hell would break loose. My job was to remind Sarelle that Olivia was a child and to help her back off. It's not an easy task with a career narcissist. What was hard and a painful reminder was that mom's behavior mimicked what I had received when I was Olivia's age. It was difficult to observe, but it was also quite reaffirming, in a therapeutic way, that all the treatment I had received from her I hadn't somehow exaggerated.

It was on one of those occasion that Olivia leaned over to me and asked why her grandma always had to be right and I told her I would explain it to her later. Which I did. Which I always did when she had difficult questions. That kind of dialogue has been one of the great flagships of my relationship with my daughter. I have to say, she is now eleven and the questions can border on the provocative. Sometimes bordering on inappropriate. Where do kids her age get this stuff from? I think the more lascivious questions are influenced by social media and also movies. It's amazing what is discussed in supposed PG films. And though me and Lois monitor her YouTube watching (she cannot watch TikTok), I am sure there are morsels that slip through. Not to mention the songs she listens to. She is a Justin Beiber and Taylor Swift fanatic (a Swiftie, she would correct me if she were reading this), and the allusions in their songs can really push the envelope. I am the censor who skips songs in the car when the F- bomb or other illicit content appears, but there are times when she is alone, and I am sure she sneaks certain content we have outlawed, despite all the parental controls. What I so cherish is that Olivia comes to me with anything. I never shame her or shut her down, and she knows that. I'm always interested in what is going on with her and what is on her mind, and she knows that. She always fezzes up even when she knows she has done something not cool. It might take her some time, but her sense of honesty always wins in the end. I tell her that I am proud of her a lot. Her integrity and empathy are two of her flagships. And when we have a fight, we are able to come back to each other and talk it through. We are able to find peace every time. The one thing I practice, which was not offered to me as a child, is apology. When I do something wrong, I will always own it. And she knows that.

Back to her and my mother. Many times, a loving snuggle in the back seat of the car devolved into a fight between a child and an adult child. I assumed my role of referee from the chauffeuring position. My eighty-year-old mom and my six-year-old daughter. In some deeply emotional ways, my mother's childhood wounds prevented her from evolving past six. These scraps were revelatory. I had been raised in many ways by a six year old.

Despite all the hijinx, my daughter and mother adored each other. I believe with as much certainty as is possible, that my daughter gave my mother a reason to live in the latter years of her life. She was seventy-six when Olivia appeared and eighty-five when she died. Even with a decline in health I think she would have referred to those nine years as among the best of her life. And all that time spent brought her and I immeasurably closer. It was a beautiful time. Many positive memories.

Sarelle's death really crept up gradually and then all at once. Her progressive back problems that worsened in her late seventies prevented her from driving long distances and relegated her to the couch most of the day. She endured and recovered from Lymphoma in her early seventies, suffered from irritable bowel syndrome, once had poison ivy that lasted months, was sensitive to practically any injection she ever took, including the Covid injections, but she was sharp as a tack and deeply engaged in her life despite all these limitations. One of our great common grounds was the New York Mets. She had been a huge New York baseball Giants fan growing up in the Bronx, attending games with her father at the old Polo Grounds, and when the Giants, like the Dodgers fled the city for the sunny climes of California, this left a void for all National League fans. The Mets filled that void in 1962, the year I was born. Though originally a laughable outfit, most of those abandoned fans flocked to the Mets. Those early Mets were basically the Harlem Globe Trotters of Major League Baseball, a clown show. The rule is that when an expansion team is formed, every other team has to give up one player to the new franchise. Of course, they give their most dispensable player- either not very good by Major League standards or over the hill. In those early days, I was not conscious enough to appreciate how laughable the team was and what a miracle their winning the 1969 World Series just seven years later was. I came of age as a sports fan that year. It was arguably the most memorable year in New York sports. The Mets and the football Jets were national champs. And in an overlapping season into 1970, the New York Knicks followed suit. I have become a lifelong devotee of all three teams. For years up until the year my mother died, we would call each other whenever there was very good or very bad news about the Mets. There were many times we would call each other right after a big win. It was a real sweet spot for us. To this day, my impulse is to pick up the phone when there is Met-worthy news.

My mother had an odd blood reading in the spring of 2021. After further investigation, the doctors found a growth in her pancreas. After a battery of tests and an eventual biopsy, cancer was confirmed. That confirmation came in late August. By mid-October she was gone. The growth had progressively blocked off her ability to digest food and eventually to urinate, requiring the assistance of tubes at both ends. Shortly thereafter, bile began backing up in her body, and she needed a surgical procedure to relieve the poisonous fluid. It was at this point that she had enough. Still of sound mind, albeit enduring tremendous pain, she decided to have all of the tubes that were keeping her alive removed. An incredibly brave choice. A week later, she died in hospice.

Jewish tradition requires burying the dead quickly, with no open casket wake. The pre-burial service occurred in a nondenominational funeral home, the same one that handled my stepfather's burial the year before. When we got to the chapel, the casket was opened. We are not a highly religious family, but this was definitely unusual. The funeral director said we could close it if we wished, but many families like to have it open for close family members, and when the guests started to arrive, they would close it. This was novel, but I like novel, so we went with it. My daughter spent the most amount of time next to her grandmother. At one point, I said to her,

 "Honey, you don't have to stay next to her if it's disturbing you," to which she replied,

"I want to. It's the last time I will see Grandma." Heartbreaking.

My mother's death had a deep and lasting impact on Olivia. She and her grandma had an inexplicable connection. But aren't all connections inexplicable on some level? This connection overrode whatever difficulties they experienced together.

I fully expected my mother's death to throw me into a tailspin, the same as my dad's death did twenty-five years earlier. I grieved, but I remained steady. The only irrefutable explanation for this newfound steadiness in crisis was the Lamictal, the mood stabilizer that had been prescribed for bipolar disorder. This was a hugely encouraging sign for my life. Would I never have another episode? The spectre of my father's failed attempts at lasting relief from medicine always lurking. It's been almost four years since my last collapse, incited by a trauma. The trauma of my mother's death did not catalyze a collapse.

Despite my mom's very questionable behavior towards me and my brother well into our twenties, she might just be the unlikely heroine of this story. In her later years, I considered her a confidante and dear friend (with some serious pauses… remember the Chanukah story. LOL). For the most part, I stopped feeling judged by her. Over the years, I have come to appreciate how her strength, under the withering oppression of my father's illness, kept us with a roof over our heads. The scene of me as a thirteen-month-old in the backseat of our red Chevy, my thirty-two year old dad in the middle of his first nervous breakdown, my mother driving him to the hospital, enduring all the crises virtually without any support, has defined her strength and courage for years. Any day my father could have done something or forgot to do something to lose his job. For example, some rowdy students set a fire in the back of his classroom. How did he not catch that? And how did he not get fired, then? Any day he could have ended up back in the hospital. How he retained his public teaching job for twenty long years escapes me, but living with that daily uncertainty must have been staggering for them both. We heard that my father had been protected by the assistant principal at the last junior high where he taught. This administrator liked my dad and knew or suspected my father's condition. If he got three unsatisfactory reviews he would have been fired. Before he was about to get that final "U," he brokered a deal with the Principal that they would hold off giving Carl that "U" and when my father hit his pension year, he would retire. My mother had been forced to leave teaching when she became pregnant with me (a controversial policy ended after a fight with the teacher's union in the 1970s), so the family depended on my father's earnings. Though that retirement was the beginning of the end for my dad, his pension and disability checks kept us going until my mother got herself back into the workforce. For those twenty years, day-to-day survival required her to captain the ship with her characteristic strength and steely resolve. I don't remember her being depressed one day in her life. Thank God for that. At least there was one non-depressed person in the house.

****

Back to my burgeoning post-separation/divorce relationship. Once we were two immunization and two boosters into COVID and the case numbers plateaued at their lowest level in two years, I nervously reached out to Hannah and floated the idea of us seeing each other again, with no expectations but no masks and no geographic restrictions. To my amazement, she answered with an unqualified yes. Of course, I leaped into the future in my mind. Was this a trial? Could we access the power we had once shared? I knew all too well from my marriage how relationships morph, and sometimes people move in different directions. Of course, there was the wild card, my mental health, to grapple with.

As it turned out, the electricity was still there, and so was the romantic flame. We slid into bed like we had never left it, echoes of our first night of lovemaking under that luminescent moon. At breakfast the next morning, she initiated the relationship talk. She was still in love with me and wanted to pick up again. The mental illness thing didn't really bother her as I was clearly being upfront about being responsible with my treatment, but she had begun a polyamorous lifestyle and needed to continue exploring it. Polyamory? Why had she taken up with someone else, more than one someone else, given all her COVID stipulations? Were all these men and women cohabitating in her home?

I confronted her in my new, healthy, non-confrontational demeanor. She revealed that she had met a man, a doctor at the hospital where she worked as a therapist. She had returned to work in person two months prior and was lonely. Apparently, it was a relationship that, according to her, "surprised" them both. OK. That happens. It has happened to me. And she insisted that she didn't know where things stood with me.

"Why didn't you ask?"

"I don't know. With all the time that had elapsed, I thought that maybe you had moved on."

"How many other partners do you have?" I asked

"One or two others, but they aren't serious at all."

"You never struck me as a casual sex kind of

person." "I'm not. I wasn't. I'm giving this a try."

"Does this have anything to do with my condition," I pressed.

"No, not at all. It just… happened," she insisted.

"A surprise."

"Absolutely."

I felt my new healthy communication style fraying. My defenses started rising and with good reason. My paranoia about her reaction to my illness only heightened my distrust of her responses. I didn't buy it... I was lonely, too, and reluctantly agreed to try. In polyamory, the belief is that jealousy is a primitive emotion and that those with advanced evolution- the polyamorists- had surmounted jealousy and opened themselves to loving any number of partners. It wasn't about sex. It was about love, they claimed. In one configuration of polyamory, such as this one, one person is the primary lover, and then others who enter the network are satellites to that central relationship. Naturally, I thought I would at least sit at the center of this galaxy. Ou contraire. Apparently, the doctor had supplanted me. I was relegated to an orbit. I suppose, in their view I was a Cro-Magnon when it came to relationships. I have and likely always will be a monogamist, possibly a serial monogamist, but a monogamist nonetheless. I engaged the experiment with a fair degree of pessimism.

A month later, already challenged by the setup, I had an experience that I was sure was proof that destiny had revealed itself. I was wrapping up a screenplay that dealt with, of all things, polyamory. This was an adaptation of a play that had been written years before and optioned for a motion picture. I was in the eye of that story or a related version of that story. The real kicker was that in her therapeutic work, Hannah was starting to experiment with psychedelics as a method of treatment. She, being a responsible practitioner, had begun experimenting with psychedelics herself. To "experience what her clients might experience." Apparently Mr. Primary had also introduced her to this world as well. Her constant attempts to get me to join her in her experimentation bore no fruit. In my early thirties I attended a Buddhist teaching with the Dalai Lama. He was initiating a hall with "the largest Buddha on the East Coast." That day, I decided to join the Buddhist tribe and receive the Five Precepts, in my opinion, a much more humane version of the Ten Commandments with no shoulds or ifs or Angry Gods attached. One of those precepts had to do with abstaining from all intoxicants because they would cloud the mind. I needed to escape my debauchery diversions, so I dove in completely.

As already mentioned, from age thirty-three to fifty-seven, I was completely abstinent of all and every, I mean every, substance. I was never a huge experimenter when it came to heavy drugs, and I didn't really care for the taste of beer. A close cousin begged me to try a wine he loved, and I swished it around my mouth and then spit it out. When I do anything, I'm all in.

On a night in the spring of 2021, the producer/director (who optioned one of my plays for a film) and I were working on the adaptation in his East Village apartment, snacking throughout, and decided to call it quits at around eleven with another writing session planned for the morning. During that time, I was customarily waking up in the middle of the night at least once, and it would take me a bit to fall back asleep. A little food in my belly always helped. This night was no different. Around four am, I awoke, went to the fridge, and grabbed something to eat. A half-hour later, still awake, the phone I was looking at began to fade in and out and moved back and forth. I got scared. I could barely stand but I went to the bathroom to splash my face and drink water. It didn't help. I finally decided that if I was going to die, then I should at least ask for help. Jim, the producer, lives in an old fashion railroad apartment, a long apartment going from the front of the building all the way to the back. The walk from the living room where I was sleeping all the way to the front of his place where he was asleep felt like an odyssey. I finally arrived and rapped on the door. Jim was pissed. It was not quite five am, and he had told me specifically not to wake him up until eight-thirty.

"I'm not feeling well, Jim."

"Go back to sleep," he

groaned.

"I had Botox put in my jaw for

clenching." No answer.

"I also had Novocain and maybe something I ate, combined with---"

"I don't know shit about Novocain. Go back to bed!"

"I also ate something out of the fridge… It was chocolate."

Jim lept out of bed and, in what seemed like a nanosecond, was right in my face.

"How much did you eat?"

He ran past me towards the kitchen. What was it that I had eaten? Any guesses? Mushrooms. And a lot of them. One dose is one square of chocolate. I had eaten seven. I was in the middle of my first psychedelic trip and had inadvertently broken my intoxicant precept, though being hijacked by a drug, I'm sure, doesn't count. Jim contacted the friend who gave him this bar of chocolate and researched the potential dangers of ingesting this high dose online. It turned out that I wasn't in danger.

"Relax and enjoy the trip," Jim said. How was I supposed to do that?

The kicker of this episode arrived in an early morning text. I thought for sure God had intervened on behalf of my relationship. Hannah, my polygamous pseudo-partner, had just woken up and sent me a text about the positive impacts that psychedelics were having on patients. What?? I was in the middle of what they call a non-realism experience, where I could not trust that anything I was saying, seeing, or hearing was real. One of the effects of the mushrooms. It was easy to believe that this text was another psychedelic-induced fantasy. I had to ask Jim to look at the message to make sure it was actually there. It was. Hannah had never sent me a message that early in the morning. Ever.

Jim responded to the text for me and explained everything about what I was in the middle of. Hannah immediately called, and Jim spoke with her. They went back and forth, she asking questions. He provides answers. She had confirmed what he had already learned. I would not die or suffer from brain erosion. He handed me the phone, and she offered loving comfort, and texted me music- special mushroom trip music? - And reassured me I'd be ok. Before she hung up, she, like Jim, encouraged me to relax and try to enjoy the trip.

What would have been if this wasn't the universe speaking, confirming our love and union? But nowhere in that spiritual message was an assurance of long-lasting monogamy. One month later, I ended things. Just too painful. The last time I had lain awake obsessing about who the girl I was into might be sleeping with was in my early twenties.

Recently we started texting again, and I learned that she had given up polyamory. Soon after, she invited me to visit her in Costa Rica, which is where she remains as a yoga teacher following a long-term teacher training.

I am still deciding whether to go or not. How many rounds can you go with one person? And I am not planning on moving to Costa Rica, as wonderful as I hear it is.

****

A year before my mother died, my stepfather Joe passed.

The little secret surrounding my mother and stepfather's relationship…

Not so alarming initially but more so later and then less so after that- my stepfather was my mother's psychiatrist on and off for many years. The boundary smearing that began in my childhood continued apace. But if this delicate situation could be handled respectfully and caring, that is how Joe handled it. Sometime after my parents separated, he told my mother he had feelings for her and had to discontinue their therapy. A month or so later, they had their first date. My mother confided in me and asked for my advice which was certainly more inappropriate boundary- crossing. Additionally, I was still reeling from my father's departure. In my innocence and desire for my mom to be happy, I encouraged her to go on a date.

"Just check it out, Mom. He's not asking you to marry him." Six months later, he moved in, and a year later, they were married.

I liked him a lot initially, and I think he liked me, but any child who is caught in the web of their parents' divorce would likely have a hard time if a new man was suddenly moving in and sleeping in the same bed where you were conceived and your father slept your entire life. I am sure his being my mom's former therapist contributed to my discomfort. It was all so confusing. My mother was grounded for the first time since the separation, and Joe's job as assistant director of a prominent psych department put our family in an income bracket we had never been close to.

After time, the absurdity of their meeting faded, but given his position of authority in her life, the shifting of their power dynamic has always seemed quite ironic.

The biggest shock of that period was how the dynamic between my mom and I shifted. After my father left, I became the so-called man of the house. Appropriate or inappropriate, my mother shared everything with me. She was vulnerable, sad, and scared. She relied on the consistency of my support. The dynamic shifted as soon as Joe became a fixture in her life. She resumed her tough love stance and all the softness and vulnerability vanished. Suddenly, she was the mother, and I was the child again. As inappropriate as the confidante relationship was, her softness felt good. That version of my mother vanished with Joe's arrival, not to be seen again until much later in her life when I was in the middle of my own separation and divorce.

Instability on top of instability.

My stepdad was a relatively reserved man. He was incredibly smart, maybe even genius smart, an assistant director of a dangerous psych ward most of his professional life, and had a very good heart. But then there were irrational bursts of rage, shades of my father. I had enough of all that mercurial treatment—feeling care, then suddenly having to defend myself. The state of anticipating and dissecting irrationality returned.

I left their home, my home, the day after they married, a month before my eighteenth birthday, weeks before my first day of college. An escape I desperately needed but was far from ready for. Turned out, some four years later, two years after I entered Alanon, shortly after his sixty-ninth birthday in the midst of their marriage-threatening fighting, Joe admitted his lifelong alcoholism. We were Jews. What did we know about alcoholism?

I have come to know Jews in both AA and Alanon, but we are certainly in the vast minority. The drink was never something that was commonplace in our homes. At celebrations, sure, but mainly the sugared-up Manischewitz that no one drank in excess. There wasn't one awful drunken scene from my early childhood with my dad. The first was at a step-family function that resulted in my twelve-year-old brother under a restaurant bathroom hand drier drying his hair after being plied by my stepbrothers with Dinkel Aker beer. But even then, I didn't log that as a symptom of alcoholism. It was just wacky older brother-younger brother fun with a few newly acquired older brothers participating. But there Joe was, knocking on seventy, entering the rooms of AA, and if there was ever an AA success story, he was it.

The man made meetings five or six days a week for twenty-four years. He was one of the most celebrated former drunks in those rooms. A die-hard until his death at ninety-four, he was affectionately referred to as Doc. He was so loved there that in his final years, when he couldn't drive himself to meetings, there was always someone from the program volunteering to take him to a meeting- for every meeting! The program did for him what it does for all folks who truly commit to it. It restores them to sanity and the people they really are. It did this to me and also my mom from the Alanon side.

But the alcoholic years co-existing with him and my mother were very difficult. More so on my brother, who lived with them for eight years before he went off to college. I endured two. Joe didn't say much, especially when my mother acted irrationally and accusatively. Clearly, he didn't want to challenge his new wife. My brother and I looked to him for support, but none was forthcoming. That was hard and set us against him for quite a number of years. Isn't the person standing silent around explicit abuse just as culpable, an accessory? What's worse is that it felt like he knew how inappropriate her behavior was, how harmful, but chose to do nothing. In ways, those years felt as dangerous as many with our mentally ill father's pre-physical violence. No ally, no witness acknowledging the behavior, and, at times, adding his own brand of rage. To cap that off, I was told after a couple of years home after I transferred to NYU that they would no longer be paying for my therapy. I guess I wasn't becoming who they wanted me to be fast enough. For the sake of my self-preservation, I moved into my own place when I came back to New York from Brandeis University, a place I never belonged in the first place. Too small, too remote, too cliquish. I began working full-time at my cousin's Bronx-based business to pay the bills and went to NYU at night. Perhaps my mother and Joe were hurt and resentful that I didn't want to live with them; perhaps this was their latest version of tough love, I don't know. But paying for my own therapy actually turned out to be a good thing. I largely did my best to avoid them both. My cousin

Alan's employment and friendship were a buffer for those many years between my parents' insanity and my recovery. He understood, supported, and saw my folks' behavior for what it was. This was the validation I had longed for, and it gave me the courage to remain faithful to my choice to keep my distance from them. In many ways, he became the fall guy. My mother never forgave him for what she perceived as his poisoning my relationship with her—another example of my mother's inability to take responsibility for her absurd behavior. I am grateful to Alan for willingly defending me all those years and providing me with steady work and support while studying acting. He was truly my first reliable consistent family ally.

Monumental how dedicated AA/Alanon's recovery changed everything for them and between us. After living for all these years as our worst selves to enjoy over twenty years as our progressively best selves was quite something, the wreckage of our past more and more a distant memory. I still never forgot their crimes lest I drop my guard all the way down, but ones that informed our daily lives less and less. Joe and I, for those twenty years, enjoyed each other's company, celebrated the arrival of my daughter, and rooted for the same sports teams we watched at a stadium or on TV. He was filled with unbelievable stories: his time serving during WWII and discovering the GI Bill, without which he could never have afforded college. His rejection at every US medical school he applied to and his acceptance into the med school in Padova, Italy. His tales of watching every English and Italian dubbed or subtitled movie he could watch to learn the Italian language. Can you imagine wrestling with a medical textbook without knowing the language? He graduated alongside all the other native speakers. Truly remarkable. I have tremendous gratitude and respect for him.

It turned out Joe was an unexpected role model. Not of all characteristics, but when it came to ingenuity, smarts, and perseverance, he was somewhere near the top of the list.

I have wondered why he never identified my bipolar, or at least depressive tendencies, as a formidable psychiatrist. Perhaps he didn't want to intrude- I was also a very skillful hider- or maybe he was too lost in his alcoholism to manage anything outside his own life. Denial, which all alcoholics suffer from, is a powerful consciousness alterer. Entering a new family, he likely didn't want to accept that both of his stepsons-to-be were afflicted by some degree of mental illness. Later, he would have to accept that two of his three birth sons, my step-brothers, also suffered from alcoholism. Joey, the eldest, died of this disease at sixty years old, jaundiced from head to toe. Joey died a year before Joe did, and we are sure that his eldest son's death hastened his own.

Joe's decline in health was progressive, but his death seemed to happen all at once. A chest cold followed by an explosive bout of coughing- he suffered from COPD after a lifetime of smoking- and then by pneumonia. A stint followed a long hospitalization in an adult home/rehab. He had followed this identical course before in the last six or seven years of his life, short of pneumonia. This time in rehab, he got worse, not better. One morning, my stepbrother Michael found him nonresponsive and unaware of the do-not-resuscitate order; Joe was rushed to the hospital. He quickly fell into a coma and was immediately intubated. A familiar scene from my own father's demise. Mercifully, it took my mother and my two step-brothers a matter of hours to honor his wishes and remove the breathing support.

Hours later, he was gone.

I miss him. The sober Joe became a friend and a loved one. Not quite a father, but pretty close. In the years since he became sober, he became loquacious at times, a far cry from the silent man I knew from my childhood. I looked forward to seeing him and hearing all his stories even if some of them I'd heard at least ten times. They were still fascinating and heroic, and at each telling, a new detail or two would emerge, as if this repetition was shaking some memory free. He loved my mother, and she loved him. It wasn't the kind of relationship I aspired to, but it worked for them. They were life companions and helped each other. He loved to travel and introduced my mother to many exotic locations by sea and air. And, of course, they shared their passion for the Mets!

****

How did I find my way to the forgiveness of my three parents? It's a sometimes baffling and complex question. I think the most direct path was the one to my dad, Carl. Although emotionally, there was a lot of work to do, bleeding out all the pain from years of disappointment and hurt, forgiving him made the most sense. He had a horrible disease. When I could fully accept that, it was hard to hold him accountable for all of his actions. When he was in an episode, he would become a completely different person. He wasn't an angel when he was in a more balanced place, but he was quite fun, well-intentioned, kind, and lovable. This paved a clear path toward forgiveness.

My mom was a lot harder because her behavior persisted deep into my adult years, beyond her divorce and well into her years of marriage to Joe. I don't know if forgiveness would have been possible if Joe and then she hadn't found their Twelve Step programs. Soon after she began, the tools of the program started arresting the worst of her damaging behavior and, over time, helped curtail most of the rest. She, like Joe, in large part, recovered her essential self. As mentioned, she could still be extremely difficult at times, but those times were much less frequent, and her care and love came forth much more readily and with greater ease. My own recovery, which was having the same effect on me, brought out my compassion for her and her own childhood struggles, which were formidable. We were able to find mutual respect for each other and even happiness in each other's company for the first time since I was a toddler. That happiness persisted to the day she died. She was still her irascible self, but it became less of an issue as I began to find my own center and confidence.

With Joe, it was a much easier path. He was my stepfather and appeared when I was fifteen. I left the house when I was eighteen, never to return again, so there was much less damage to forgive. I have recounted the ways in which his pre-recovery behavior took its toll on me and especially my brother, but for me, Joe's damage was wrought more by omission. He always felt like the supporting character until later when, in recovery, he emerged as a friend and central character. And again, I have tremendous compassion and empathy for those who are and were struggling with a disease, in this case, alcoholism. So, the path to forgiving him was made easier by his accepting of his illness. He never apologized to me or, to my knowledge, to my brother, but for me, his amends were made in his newer, more open, caring, and interested behavior.

Forgetting is an entirely other matter. In Alanon, it is said, "Look back, but don't stare." Looking back is essential. Equally as important is letting go. But forgetting would mean a blind sense of trust, which I never had with any of them when they were alive. Yes, I could love and trust them all to a certain extent, but the knowledge of what they were capable of was always present. On some level, there was always vigilance, an element of self-protection. In the case of my mother and father, this was necessary. Even in their later years, they were both capable of mercurial, irrational, and explosive behavior. Not so much my stepfather. He was steadier and more reliably consistent. I was pleased to see him find his voice and stand up to my mother more as he got older.

Remembering references where I come from and what I have endured and come through. The strength, faith, and endurance I possess. Many would not have made it out of that home capable of leading productive and balanced lives. I found my way. It was impossibly fraught at times, times when I really thought I wouldn't make it, that I would be subsumed by my pain and my own maladies. Remembering keeps me humble, most days appreciative. I am grateful for the person I have become, and it would be naïve and wrong to believe the trials I endured have not formed me. Grateful for the trials? I haven't gotten there all the way. I see how the wisdom of my coming through helps others, and I am grateful for that. But grateful for having lived through that? I haven't gotten there yet. Those memories are touchstones, lest I forget where I come from and what I have come through.

****

I wanted my brother Andrew's perspective on all of this so we scheduled another Zoom meeting. He corroborated much of what I have written, and he crystallized events that I was blurry on.

The event in the kitchen when my father had him cornered and I grabbed Dad around his arms, leaving black and blue welts, was clear to both of us. He spoke of the many nighttime fights between our mother and father. Not that I needed reminders of that, but over the course of those fights, which got progressively worse as time went on, lying awake in bed, I started blocking them. I would put a pillow over my head and somehow fall asleep. As the older brother, I would go into their bedroom for a while and try to settle things down. But at some point, I stopped intervening. I suppose the futility and the danger led me to a silent admission of defeat. At that point, Andrew stepped into that role. He recalls beckoning me for help, but I wouldn't come. My brother said that only when the fights escalated towards physical violence did I emerge, but I don't remember most of that either. Writing this now, I remember the tone change of the fight and our mother starting to scream as our dad drew closer to her.

I must have unconsciously recalled chunks of this as I wrote a play centered around my dad's illness when in the middle of one of those blowouts, the brother inadvertently stepped in front of the father's punch, which killed him. Fictional, but in reality, that threat always existed.

What was true in the play and also refreshed in the Zoom talk with my brother was how incessant our mother's badgering of our father was. Despite her deep involvement in his care, her rage at whatever innocuous issue they were fighting about trumped any compassion or awareness of what backing a severely mentally ill man prone to violence into a verbal corner would lead to. As discussed, she was a much more skilled elocutionist than my dad. He had street smarts but was not facile verbally. Her onslaught would inevitably lead to his defending himself with his fists. Apparently, what would get me out from under my pillow was the imminent threat of my father ending up on top of her, restraining her, and intermittently striking her. The number of times I pulled him off of my mother is still in question. My mother used to say nine or ten times, my brother recollected less. In either case, I only remember doing it once. Repressed memories that I still cannot recall.

These questions have appeared for the first time while writing this at the age of sixty-one: Is it possible that my retreat from those fights and my subsequent unwillingness to intervene had to do with my disgust at how my mother was treating him? On some level, did I feel that she deserved to be shut up? Not only in that moment but for all the moments she abused all of us verbally?

My brother didn't fare as well. He has carried hurt and resentment beyond her passing. I believe that the main reason he left for California in his late thirties was to escape her fast trigger finger and my stepfather's taking my mother's side. Well into Andrew's late forties and her old age, they could still provoke each other into verbally violent fights. As recounted earlier, one night, when my brother flew in during one of my stepfather's late-in-life hospital stays, he and our mom got into a battle royale, leading to her kicking him out in the middle of the night. After that occurrence, they didn't speak for close to two years, and when enough time had passed- neither could apologize- and my brother resumed visiting, he would stay at nearby hotels rather than test the fates sleeping under her roof. The only and last time he stayed in that apartment again was in the two weeks leading up to her death. She was in the hospital the entire time.

****

It would have been easy to have lived my life as a victim. One doesn't choose the home life to grow up in, and if one does, as some believe, then I needed to learn some harsh lessons. I never really bought into the lemonade out of lemons thing particularly when a period of one's life feels mostly like being pelted by lemons, but I can see and appreciate how coming through what I have has provided me with skills and perhaps gifts that others might not possess.

I had no choice in my home but to develop a very keen sense of awareness- hypervigilance- in an environment that could and did become emotionally or physically violent at any time, provoked or unprovoked. To this day I can walk in and pretty quickly read a room. I intuitively sense where potential danger could lie.

I have always been very curious about what makes people tick. Likely borne out of a natural curiosity, this quality was amplified by the exposure at a young age to the darker side of being human. Most kids, thankfully, aren't exposed to this brand of psychopathy. Rather than become overwhelmed by it all or block it out, I sought answers that thrust me into a deep study of humans. The need to see, to know sparked a taste for inquiry. This search broadened into the spiritual realm and activated what would become one of the great adventures of my life which led my search to India, Nepal, and Rome. Maybe that taste was inbred already, but my circumstances undoubtedly liberated it. My most satisfying conversations with friends or girlfriends were always ones that penetrated the mundane. On this exploration, I met many like-minded travelers, and discussions delving into motivation, ulterior motives, obstacles to behavior, and wounds became commonplace. As geographically prohibitive as this relationship would become- she lived in California- Cassidy appeared when I was twenty. The only significant connection that was borne out of a New York City dance club meeting and who is still a dear friend today. She was a Buddhist and a writer, and we reveled in shared inquiry. This common necessity was magnetic and turned the sex electric. It became the new standard not only for sexual partners but for relationships in general. This newly discovered tribe was not content with accepting conventional understanding. We needed to probe, debate, and draw our own conclusions. We were post-hippie, yippee, flower child, sexual liberation, and at the tail end of women's lib. I did catch the wave of the 90's men's movement, which was important, but brief. This tribe was more universal than any one movement. I am glad that there were no bandwagons to attach ourselves to. It was a simple credo, the pursuit of truth, which fit perfectly with my early twenties introduction to acting, as truth in that field was always and remains true north.

Truth is elusive and, in many instances, subjective, to be sure, but when one is in the middle of it on stage, it is undeniably exhilarating to exist in or to witness. It was visceral and imaginary. Mind, body, voice. A full-bodied experience. Steve, my dear friend and one of my first important theatre collaborators, claimed a phrase: "The Shining Star." It came from a monologue by Eric Bogosian who was revolutionizing the one- person-show in downtown Manhattan theatres in the 80's. The term, as we understood it, referred to one's highest truth. The quest, to reach that star, artistically, personally, became our religion.

I am not a therapist, but I have been told by many that acting training has therapeutic value. It certainly did for me. Facing demons and fears are requisites on the acting path. If we can't face these, we can't inhabit the roles that require bringing those aspects of ourselves to the fore. My folks were both teachers. It is a profession that, at its best, requires seeing into the students' humanity as much as their minds. In its highest form, teaching asks us to participate in developing all the lives we teach. Combine that with the acute seeing training I acquired as a child, and that is quite a lot of seeing. I love it. I always have. When the room is held in this way, and the students know and feel it, the journey takes on magical and profound proportions. The students begin opening up to themselves and each other, and personal transformation can begin. I have witnessed life-altering openings in my acting classes. There is no other way, in my opinion. We bring who we are to each role in whatever state of openness we occupy. The more open, the more available we are to the panoply of emotions and experiences.

Another quality I possess is a heightened sense of empathy for those in the midst of emotional challenges which means most of us. As mentioned earlier, I have a special place in my heart for those afflicted with handicaps - individuals on the spectrum, those who suffer from mental illness, and those afflicted by other emotional or psychological challenges. These folks seem to find me, and I them. I like to think that I bring a unique understanding of the perceived and actual alienation that these conditions engender. All we want is to be accepted for who we are in our "Full Catastrophe," the phrase coined by John Kabat-Zin, including all of our problems, defeats, and handicaps. I have always known how to do that, I am sure, because of living with and loving my dad. Despite the horrendous behaviors caused by his illness, I was always able to see and feel the beauty of him. This is one of the reasons we were so close.

****

I have been obsessed with my career since I discovered acting in my mid-twenties. Becoming the best craftsman I could be, making a livable wage, which eludes many artists, and being recognized by my peers and the wider world. When I felt behind, not getting where I thought I should be, my go-to obsession was how my family had held me back and down. I wasn't interested in acting when I was a kid, so literal discouragement for this life choice didn't appear, not until later. It was growing up in a war zone that stunted my development. Every choice living inside all that was a strategy not an organic decision.

****

In our recent phone call, my brother told me that right around the time I was leaving the house for college, he was crying every day. Clearly, his depression and despair were escalating. My leave-taking and his being left alone in all of that likely exacerbated his feelings. He told me that while he was crying, he would hide behind one of the couches in the living room. He was looking for privacy and probably knew no solace was available. The kill shot came from my stepfather, who was in the throes of his alcoholism, about which we knew nothing at the time, and was also newlywed to our mother. He told my brother, "If you don't stop crying, I'm going to put you into the oven." My brother tells me that after that moment his tear vault slammed. He hasn't shed another tear since. Horrible. The power of a parental threat.

It took me another seven years of painstaking, desperate

searching to discover what I was meant to be and do. Amazing that while cycling in and out of despair, I could finish school, pay rent, and find my path. As I was beginning to compete as an actor and then director, my starting later than most in a young person's game became an obstacle. Actors who had been acting since they were in their adolescence, some younger, many who had gone to highly touted collegiate and graduate programs, had more than a leg up on a twenty-seven-year-old upstart.

For years and decades, I blamed my falling short of the recognition I so coveted as an actor, director, and then writer on my arrested start in life. This may have been true, but holding to that belief did nothing but make me more miserable. With the start I had in life and the mental illness I inherited, there was an abundance of justifications for victimhood. In a retreat I attended, led by a seasoned and skilled therapist I had worked with for years, all the participants were asked to tell their life stories in five minutes. A daunting task. Each of us got up and told the story as victims of the abuses and wrongs visited upon us. Each person certainly had a right to see their life through that part of the prism. After the last one of us told their story, we took a break, and when we came back, we were asked to tell our story again, but this time to tell them about the hero's journey. This was a revelation. The new tales celebrated the strength and determination each person possessed in overcoming all of our formidable obstacles. After that weekend, something shifted within me. Not that I still didn't bemoan my upbringing- there was still plenty more work to do bleeding those wounds- but there was now a space within me that could see how my perspective on life, given where I came from, was unique and later, how the stories I began telling had value for others.

As an acting teacher, I had known for a long time that this was the case. I was able to guide students through their own journeys and face their fears through the medium of acting—art as a crucible. I can't minimize artistic exploration and expression's role in my healing process. I see that clearly when I witness the benefit for the people I teach. It really is a beautiful gift to behold and the most significant outcome of turning my sorrow and pain into a force of aid. I used to see teaching acting as a sidebar, a survival job secondary to my own artistic practices. It took many years, probably until my early fifties, to fully accept and celebrate all the ways I was, as Michael Howard, my master teacher, coined, "turning the shit of my life into gold." On some level, all artmaking has an element of this in it. Perhaps for some more than others. I would say that the first ten plays I wrote were an exorcism of sorts. Saying what needed to be said on the page that had needed to be told for years. Playwriting grew out of a frustration with directing: the stories I wanted to tell weren't contained in the vast number of published plays I had read or the new plays that were being sent to me by my agent. I needed to tell my own stories—such an amazement to have found that I had an aptitude for that form of writing.

The last remnants of suffering around career recognition were eradicated by COVID-19. Occasionally, there are still stirrings of jealousy and resentment, but nothing that lasts particularly long. Obsession is a bad neighborhood to hang out in so I use as many tools as possible to get out as fast as possible. There is definitely an obsessive component to my mental illness. It can turn my mind toward fantasy, but the thoughts' predominant direction is towards the dark. But they do come much less these days. For that, I am incredibly grateful. I have found that there were behaviors and thinking that are so deeply habitual that despite all the therapy, the Alanon, the prayer, the meditation, it felt like they would never disappear.

I have come to view suffering less as an indictment of my own life and more as an outcome of being alive. I have come to learn and accept that suffering is relative, but we all share in that aspect of life. And more often than not, there are silver linings—not always, but a lot of the time.

****

What merits further examination is my unlikely trajectory through the arts and the success I have enjoyed despite my malady and many bipolar episodes. I think of the phrase, "Make hay while the sun shines." That is what the hypomanic phases were. Haymaking. And I did, in fact, make plenty of hay. The guidance from acting to directing and finally to playwriting was my path to soul salvation. In addition to providing me with an outlet for all of my pain and confusion, it became clear that I was following a deep calling. Incredible to find one's calling at any age. The undenianle fact of what this path was became clear to me somewhere in my middle thirties. In my mid-twenties, when I started on this path, I didn't recognize it as such, but retrospect proved that it undoubtedly was. There were too many people that urged me towards this path to ignore the mandate that the Universe was providing. And the many miracles inside and out of the theatre. Some arrived like lightning bolts, others as a soft nudge. Alanon and my other spiritual practices opened my awareness to these moments that others might have written off as coincidences.

Here is one example: When I was becoming frustrated with directing and the projects I was being sent by my agent, I started considering the possibility of writing my own plays but pretty soon dismissed this notion. Writing of any kind, especially plays that are almost entirely dialogue-driven, is incredibly hard, and I had no experience at all. Then I got a call from a local high school where I taught annual acting classes to their English students after their Advanced Placement exams were done. This year their teacher wanted me to teach playwriting. I told him that I was a director and acting teacher, not a playwright. He said four words,

"You can do it."

So I went out and bought some "how-to" playwriting books and studied them. Days later, I had a meeting with a theatre when I was asked to write a play with and for my teenage students. I demurred, but they insisted. I had two or three other random theatre-friend encounters where I was referred to as a playwright. I found this odd at the time since they knew I was a director. Then, I met one of my close colleagues, the artistic director of a successful theatre in Westchester. He had just gotten off a train, and I happened to be getting a sandwich from the local deli. I gave him a lift back to his theatre. Not a minute into the ride, he said,

"When are you going to start writing plays?"

I was flabbergasted. If the Universe hadn't gotten my attention before, that statement by this trusted friend sealed the deal.

In truth, when I look back on my entire theatre life, I see an mystical presence intervening from the start. What are the chances that a successful athlete from an elite Science and Math High School with no prior experience with theatre would suddenly be introduced to acting in my early twenties? A well-known spiritual leader said that once you find your path, you should pursue it as if your hair is on fire. I had a full head of thick hair when I began, and now I am almost completely bald! Intense class study was followed by a number of acting and directing jobs which led to being signed by an acting and then a directing agent. Then I founded an acting school and theatre.

After I served twenty years as the founding director of Axial Theatre in Westchester, the theatre threw a big party for me and for the theatre's own twentieth anniversary as well. Twenty years of survival for any theatre is like sixty in dog years compared to most other industries. Statistically, start-up theatres drop like cadavers in the first three years of existence. Somehow the necessity to make the work, to make it in a certain way, and our ensemble members' relationships with each other kept us all assembled sharp, focused, and passionate. And despite departures and arrivals, passion and smarts have been a constant. And as the leader, I was certainly responsible for setting the tone. And for that I am proud, and I sheepishly accepted the honors that were bestowed on me that night. My stepfather, mother, and daughter accompanied me to the event. A full circle for my parents, having doubted and even maligned my acting and subsequent artistic path for years. Their participation in the celebration was a testimony to how far they had come in their acceptance of me and how perseverant I was. Their dysfunction and fear drove their early reactions. Their recovery and growth guided the last twenty-five years of their lives. I am so happy that we were able to share that moment together. They were incredibly proud, as was my then seven-year-old daughter. Success is a pretty effective palliative.

How have I pulled off thirty-five years in theatre, given my condition? A myriad of highs and lows, challenges both emotional and external that at the time seemed insurmountable.

But it all provides, at least to me, evidence of God or a Higher Power working in my life. Not only to carry me through the dark times but to lead me to the various tiers of recovery and guides, friends, and practitioners I needed. So many people- doctors, lovers, dear friends, theatre artists, teachers, students, and my daughter- helped me stay afloat and move forward. Validation, money, - both earned and donated- opportunities to practice my craft, others who wanted to practice and present with me, others who wanted to support the work, both paid and volunteer, and space to do the work. I do believe that what we are set on this earth to do is find support from those unseen forces if we are willing to do the necessary work. Especially when faced with huge challenges. So many drop out when the going gets really tough. I had constant doubts and fears, but always managed to stay the course. When the doubts got almost too much to bear, a person always entered my life with encouragement to keep going.

In retrospect, the hypo-manic phases prompted incredible productivity. It didn't feel unusual or superhuman at the time, but looking back on it I wonder if I could have produced half as much without that ailment. I think about Johann Wolfgang von Goethe and Leonardo da Vinci, both of whom had myriad and prolific accomplishments. Goethe: author, poet, philosopher, scientist, playwright, novelist, lawyer, diplomat, statesman, theatre director. Da Vinci: Painter, inventor, writer, mathematician, architect, engineer, sculptor, philosopher, astronomer. Geniuses as they were, where did they get the energy and time? Acting, playwriting, directing, teaching, artistic directing, producing, and entrepreneurial pursuits don't quite compare to the list of accomplishments they attained, but I recognize that it is a lot. There is suspicion that Goethe was also Bipolar. Perhaps his experience of hyperproductivity during the manic states was similar, but what about the depressive ones? Did he have fallow depressive periods followed by ones of extreme productivity? My depressive periods have been complete system shutdowns. During those phases, I would do the bare minimum and have colleagues step in for me in the administrative, directorial, and teaching capacities. I would call them leaves of absence, well-earned and much-needed breaks. They were, but they also weren't. I simply couldn't function. After the gargantuan efforts I would put in, no one seemed to question the need for rest. This was the rollercoaster I was on for years. But, despite all of that, I acted in many shows, directed many more, wrote over twenty full-length plays, founded and artistically directed a professional theatre, ran an acting studio, and taught weekly acting classes for over thirty years.

What also drove me was the desperate need for validation. A desire to get my plays out in the world to be seen by as many people as possible is natural, but the kind of desperation that motivated me was rooted far deeper. There were long periods when high praise buoyed me, and disinterest in my work triggered depressive events. I fed on praise, especially high-level praise. This feedback system was finely tuned. Great artists thinking I was great, or had the potential to be great, eventually endorsing my work, hanging out with them, getting introduced to other world-class artists by them, being recommended by them- this all turned into a dangerous drug. Any young artist would think this was the coolest and most blessed thing ever. I did meet and work with amazing artists and was welcomed into some fabulous communities as a result of those associations. But, as with any addiction, it was never enough. In fact, it only raised the threshold of satisfaction. It only worked until the next lull and then the sense of being forgotten, left behind, rose up, followed by feelings of being a nobody, a failure. The week of my first big Off-Broadway directorial debut, I woke up, grabbed a flashlight, and walked down our long driveway, the two dogs in tow, to retrieve the New York Times. Every day the important review that was certainly coming was not there. Finally, it arrived the day before the show closed. The given reason for its delayed publication was the paper's act of support for the theatre because the review turned out to be not so great. It was less an indictment of our work and more a framing of the play within the canon of this writer's other plays. Unfair. Almost three weeks of walking in the pitch black down the driveway to retrieve a review that was never there. It was excruciating. Not only because a great review would guarantee an extension of the show, but also many more high level directing opportunities. All that was painful enough, but the real problem was being so attached to the opinion in those two columns in the paper that it would define my sense of self. It defined my validity as a human. Not great for a Bipolar, not great for any human. A good review would have most certainly helped my career, but it definitely would not have made me a better, happier, more content person. Maybe it would have made me into a worse person. After the show ended, I cratered. One of the most prolonged depressions of my life.

Months after that disaster, I was offered a chance by a playwright I respected to direct one of his new plays. All was set to go when the project collapsed. The big star who was making a comeback decided to take a role in a television show. That pretty much put the kibosh on my hot pursuit of an independent directing career. So much time spent packaging projects, begging for money, or not-for-profit theatres to hire you. I was done with all of that.

At the time, I was teaching acting classes in a beautiful barn tucked away in Katonah, NY, which housed a long-standing and accomplished dance company. Concurrent with all of my directing hijinx, the dance company unexpectedly disbanded. Their artistic director was the one who owned the barn and the adjoining property. She and the other principals involved in the enterprise invited me to a meeting to determine the direction of the performance space. Since this occurred in the midst of a season, they had grant money that needed to be spent. All heads turned toward me. The invite to teach there came after a student workshop presentation of an age-appropriate play the AD had seen me direct.

"Can you create something?" "I have never written a play."

"You invented text for the show you directed them in." We did take some improvisational liberties with the play, but that was hardly creating a play from scratch.

"You can engage them in improvisation, and you'll come up with something amazing."

I finally acquiesced with the proviso that the kids would have to commit to weekly rehearsals on weekends—many of them lived a great distance—for six months, which I thought, with their busy lives, they would never be up for. These committed, talented kids jumped at the chance, essentially moving into the barn every weekend. It was an amazingly deep and searching process, indicative of the people and young artists they were.

The piece, *SWIM*, was about the effect that an alleged drowning suicide had on a band of friends. The owner-dancer of the barn helped with movement, and the guitar player from a local band that was resident at the barn composed original music. The band leader even lent her amazing voice to a song at the live performances. The entire thing was magical. There were bumps for sure, but nothing in my experience before had compared to the entire process and outcome. I wrote sections and acted as a dramaturg, which is a play editor, for the kids' writing. The performances were sold out, and demand convinced us to schedule more performances for the following Fall. A few ensemble members, who were returning to college had to be replaced, but that offered us new exploratory possibilities. I stood in the back of the audience during the first run of the show, hearing the words they had written, that we had all written, and experienced the audience's reaction and thinking, "This is what I need to do." And though I have directed since, from that point on writing became my primary path.

Life is funny and completely unpredictable. What if the Off-Broadway engagement, which took place not long before the *SWIM* process began, had been the critical success we all thought it would be? What if that star had not gotten cast in the television show and had fulfilled the next potential project we cast her in, and that play had moved to New York City? Would my writing life have ever begun? And if so, when? At the time those disappointments felt like blights, and they threw me into tailspins. I could not get my mind and heart around why that magic carpet ride and the project that introduced me so prominently to the profession would crash and burn the way it did. There were so many moments when that journey to a Manhattan premiere from Westchester seemed impossibly obstructed, but each hurdle was navigated with smarts, risk, and guile.

It certainly felt like the Unseen Hand that was guiding me and this play forward, had suddenly and cavalierly yanked everything away. Or did It? It took me many months, even several years to realize the disappointing obstruction was actually leading me into my truer life's work. It led me to co-create Axial Theatre. Despite plenty of business launching obstacles, it was undeniable that doors were opening to help the theatre along in ways that my other artistic pursuits were not. Making theatre requires a deep and wide amount of help, whether you are doing it under the roof of a permanent theatre or preparing to move from theatre to theatre. Thank God I did not spend years railing at ghosts for not delivering my playwriting brass ring and was open to the help I needed to make the theatre a success. The help came from many unlikely people. The Unseen Hand clearly had other ideas for the life I was supposed to lead.

Artistically incited disappointment. The antidote has always been to come back to myself, my prayer life, Alanon meetings, my therapist, and my relationships. Do work, and surround myself with other like-minded collaborators. But there was also the newspaper, the emergence of the internet, Facebook, and Instagram, to remind me of how many fabulous things other contemporaries were being celebrated for. This is why the first dharma talk I had heard, given by Tich Nat Hanh, was so on the nose. The potential poison is created from ingesting what we hear, read, and watch. But how could I not keep up with what was happening around me? And to feel happy and supportive of other people's, many of them colleagues' successes. It's been hard. Easier when I am in the midst of a creating wave, and near impossible when the wave is no longer a wave, barely a ripple. Of course, the news about what people are putting out is always about success unless it's about thundering failure. Which makes me feel equally as bad. Who wants failure for a friend? So there was really no place I could rest in, when learning about others' work. Someone should start a social media group for terrible news, feeling excluded on the outside, sadness, and alienation. Not as a well to languish in, but as a forum to relate, to deal and move through. I know there are plenty of others who have suffered the crushing reality of the industry's fickleness.

****

My daughter was seven or eight months old and my wife had discovered lead paint around the window sills of our turn-of-the-(last)-century converted barn rental on the apple orchard. She was finishing her MFA at SUNY Purchase, so we needed to move but remain within commuting distance of her school. An Alanon friend of mine, hearing of our plight, offered us a spacious top- floor converted attic with two rooms. Perfect. Except it wasn't. This lady and I were great Alanon friends but not-so-great housemates. We had our own bathroom but shared the kitchen and living room. Too much proximity. Too many incompatible habits. To be fair, there were plenty of lovely conversations, meals, and shared moments, but then there were the other moments. That was the backdrop from which the trip to visit my new wife's New Hampshire cousins was planned. They had never met the baby and we needed a break.

We arrived in their lovely town of Hanover, New Hampshire prepared for a first meeting with the family. All was well. Lois' cousin, the mother of the three younger cousins, was overly hospitable but in a sweet way. Nice to be pampered especially

200

with a very young child. The next day we made a visit to town for brunch. It's a nice place with delicious food. We walked the town and happened upon the campus of Dartmouth. There on the square is their theatre with a huge sign welcoming the New York City based theatre, New York Theatre Workshop, for their annual summer residency focused on exploring new works. What would have been an otherwise exciting opportunity for the average visitor for me was a major trigger. I had been a member of this theatre before I started my own theatre company and the ending had been less than auspicious. I was dropped from their roster without any warning. To this day, I don't know why.

I had never been invited to go to Dartmouth with them, though I wanted to. A few months before the New Hampshire trip and fifteen years after my ignominious departure, another of their members had applied to bring my then-newest play to this very residency. Her application had been denied. The days that followed are a blur. All I know is that I precipitously fell deeper and deeper into a depression. This kind of career-inspired depression does not follow the other pattern, where circumstantial crisis triggers fear, anxiety, and overload. This brand was like boarding an express elevator straight down to the basement. It bears mentioning that for years, each time a depression appeared on the horizon, even sometime after I began taking drugs, I still held a deeply seeded belief that I could overcome the bad feelings on my own. This habit of mind prevented me from consulting with my psychiatrist a number of time as soon as these descents began, which would have certainly resulted in an increase in the medication. By the time I finally reached out, it was too late. I had missed the window of prevention and had entered the long recovery phase.

This happened once before, a couple of months after Lois and my wedding, when I was visiting her at a Chautauqua residency in upstate New York. This super idiosyncratic gated community was equal part religious center- churches of every Christian denomination- and an elite artistic training ground for dance, fine art, and theatre. Entertainment was presented in a large covered amphitheatre as well as talks from the great minds of our times. In the same venue visiting Christian preachers would give sermons in the early morning. Not far from the amphitheater near the neighboring lakefront, there was a landscaped replica of Israel, the Promised Land, each region of the country topographically to scale. Though I subscribe to many Christian precepts, the place kind of freaked me out. Like a Christian Fellini movie. The disorientation provoked by this setting, the estrangement from my wife, and the parade of celebrity intelligentsia sent me into a tailspin. I was writing daily in a room at my wife's Chautauqua sponsor family's home. Each visiting artist was assigned a sponsor family and these folks were really cool. They tried unsuccessfully to get me a meeting with the head of the summer theatre program; the husband told a story about sitting in on bass guitar with Crosby, Stills, Nash, and Young when he was a twenty-something and the band was visiting an upstate New York venue. Clearly, this was the guy's life highlight. This man's fate pushed me further out on the edge. I didn't want to be some fucking pony-haired dude telling war stories from thirty years ago about my one brush with artistic success.

I can be in the bowels of depression and still show up for my writing or my theatre work or my classes, resistant as heck to go to the writing table, initially hating being there, somehow getting through it, and better for it at the end of the day's session. I would attend the morning sermons looking for spiritual solace.

I went every day. I think they got me through that visit. There was a powerful Black female priest who had provided ministerial council to Barack or Michelle and one of their cabinet members.

She was good, well-spoken, passionate, and spirited. One morning, she spoke of a Jewish former slave from the Old Testament fleeing with the rest of the tribe from Egyptian captivity. He had been promised by God a piece of the Promised Land to lord over. The guy was one hundred and ten, he had been living in the Holy Land for many years, and the promise had not yet been fulfilled. The message of the sermon was that God fulfilled his promise. When the man was one hundred and fifteen years old.

"Who amongst us has that kind of faith," the priest declared. "Who has enough faith in God, that they will wait that long for Him to deliver on His promise."

Even if I make it to eighty-five or ninety, who can enjoy anything in a full-bodied way at that age? Is that supposed to offer hope? Another not-so-small point is that God, to my knowledge, has never promised me anything. Being led down the path of my passion should be enough, right?

I had come to this artistic endeavor relatively late and didn't have an MFA, and even though I have been an associate at Lincoln Center and New York Theatre Workshop and co-founded a professional theatre, I have still been treated like an outsider by the industry. The MFA, over the last twenty years, has become a prerequisite for many high level opportunities. Isn't this life supposed to be about letting go of ego and committing to service? Pursuing success for success' sake is the work of the ego. Easing God Out.

"Keep making the work. The cream always rises to the top," one mentor told me.

"You can't invest in defeat. Stay angry," another mentor said.

"Life is short, art is longer," said another.

I had invested in a specific brand of anger and kept making the work. Lois would tell me that I likely wasn't a writer in my past life and discovered the talent and passion late in this life. In her view, I likely had to wait one or two more lifetimes to get my due. One of my recent ex-girlfriends studied my astrological chart and found that I would either be famous in this life or after I die. Cold comfort. At this point, I have resigned myself to post-mortem recognition. I would be in very good company.

The greatest news is that I no longer feel addicted to validation. And with the mental illness under control- God willing- I am enjoying a different phase of writing. Not driven by the promise of adulation and fame but by the pleasure of creating. Of course, I still want my work to be seen and produced, but the desperation is gone. It's such a relief not to live in hot pursuit of a mirage that would somehow save me. I have been saved but not by success. By satisfaction, by gratitude, by acceptance. I have finally taken refuge in creation, teaching, fatherhood, and friendship. I am proud and grateful for the theatre's ongoing legacy and the people the acting studio and theatre have helped. Also the opportunities it has created for many. The appreciation I periodically receive is very gratifying. The difference is that I don't need that appreciation any longer to feel good about myself.

****

What has surprisingly developed over the last several years is a deeper sense of calm and self-acceptance. Glimpses of what Alanon refers to as the priceless gift of serenity. I remain well aware of what the descent does to me, yet there is something about my lifestyle change post-Covid, including letting go of the artistic directorship of the theatre, prioritizing fatherhood, and the effectiveness of my medicinal regimen that has created new well- being and greater confidence. Somehow the running has stopped. The running towards, but more importantly, the running away from, the reality of my diagnosis. Covid broke my addiction to busyness and chasing the chalice of wider professional success and the artistic accolades I had been seeking for close to three decades. Withdrawal from all of that was incredibly painful. Gradually, what I had accomplished I began appreciating. The sense of failure lifted, as did the resentment I sometimes felt about being a career outsider, keeping me from some greater fame. But having been removed from teaching for a spell by the pandemic and then relegated to Zoom, I was desperate to get back in person with my students. There hasn't been a day since that I don't appreciate what this craft has given me, how it helps others, and what the theatre has provided and continues to provide for the community and beyond. I am proud of what has been accomplished and no longer feel that all of that is a booby prize. Of course, I hope my plays eventually reach a wider audience. And for a number of years now, I haven't had another bipolar episode. This can make some complacent about daily maintenance, skipping days of medication, or stopping the meds completely. I never fall into that trap. I know exactly what life without those drugs looks and feels like.

I don't know how long I will live—none of us do—but given the hardships I have endured, I want to live fully into my remaining time, however much of it I am granted.

Who could have predicted that it would take something as devastating as Covid to hand me all of that? A Power much greater than myself.

Pain has always been my principal motivator to seek help and change. Perhaps that is the lot for our entire species. I have had my fill of pain, but that sent me into sometimes desperate pursuit of help. Hopefully, the growth and change of my latter years can now be galvanized by the need for self-care, deeper fulfillment, and love.

I have reluctantly come to accept that I will always have a disease. And like those with diabetes, a thyroid issue, or a heart condition, mine will not go away just because I want it to. I have to respect its power, do what the doctors tell me to do, follow my spiritual path, and live my life one day at a time inside my own skin. I am certain that there will be more hard days, days when I fall prey to the disease's symptoms, but I am starting to count on the notion that there will be many more days of peace and fulfillment to relish. Amen.

That being said, some days it is hard living with this disease. It sometimes debilitates me in ways that I am unaware of, even during the best of times. The struggle with weight, often with sleep- too much or too little-forgetting to take my meds for a day. That can throw me off. Not into a full-blown depression, but into a sluggishness or mild malaise. Sticking to my morning and evening medicinal regimen is critical. Regular exercise is important, to raise the heart rate and blood flow, but also to produce those endorphins. Staying engaged with people. Not every single day, but most days. Attending Alanon meetings, parenting, teaching my classes, and seeing loved ones and friends really helps. There is very little room for kicking back and forgetting. The disease has ways of reminding me that it exists.

I also must try to maintain an accepting mindset. Accepting my lot in life has been hard but is becoming easier. Aversion, frustration, and even inner temper tantrums reinforce mybdisappointment, anger, and belief that I am a victim. As cheesy as it may sound, maintaining a sense of gratitude is key. Glass half full, as they say.

What is disappointing when I dwell on it too long, is that I will never know what a normal inner life feels like- an emotional and mental life that is uninfluenced by this condition. How do regular folk feel when they are sitting still, having conversations, working? Of course no one can ever know what it's like to live inside of another's experience. Even with all the empathy one can muster. But it is a question that does linger.

Most days, I experience a deep sense of inner fatigue; I imagine from contending with the emotional and psychic demands on my system for all these years, overworking my adrenals, debilitating depressive episodes, and thus the earlier life expectancy for people like me. I am not sure if I will ever feel spry again. This is partially a function of getting older, but also a product of having lived this life.

The only recourse is to accept what is. Do what I need to do. Get the rest that my body calls for. I am fortunate that my life presents me with space to take as much rest as I need. But- I am keenly aware of how much energy and drive I used to possess. Hard to admit that even though there are days when I am fully charged and eager to launch into the day, I am not filled with the seemingly boundless energy that would freely flow. I likely never will again. More opportunity for acceptance. I don't have to like it, but I do have to be OK with it. This is the one life I have been given and I do have much to be grateful for. Most days, I am.

Today, I choose to see my life, my journey, as a hero's journey, not a victim's. Years and years ago when I was in the midst of the worst suffering, I never thought this moment would ever arrive. What I couldn't predict back then was the arrival of so many people who would see the person I was beyond, beneath all my difficulties, and knew that with their help, I could overcome these issues. They saw that I had that hard work and determination in me long before I saw it in myself. Each of those blessed practitioners brought their special gifts and faith and helped me over many years of work through layers of grief, low self-esteem, and buckets of fear. Hundreds of hours, likely thousands of Alanon meetings, years of Buddhist practice, thirty- plus years in therapy, and a decade and a half of care from a brilliant psychiatrist.

Over time, I began to believe in myself and the healing process.

I hope whoever has taken the time to read these words can find a way to believe in their own prospect for peace and happiness. I wish that for all, suffering or not.

I hope this helps all of you who have been exposed to or afflicted by these awful conditions and anyone who is facing insurmountable obstacles. In fact, that's why I wrote this.

About the Author

Howard Meyer is a multifaceted theatre professional with extensive experience as a produced playwright, theatre director, and program director of an acting studio. As an acting teacher, he has mentored countless students, shaping their craft and preparing them for careers in the performing arts.

As a business owner, he has successfully managed both the creative and operational aspects of running a theatre company and acting school. His entrepreneurial spirit and leadership have played a vital role in sustaining and growing the organization.

He co-founded a professional theatre company and acting school, which is now celebrating its 25th anniversary season. For two decades, the theatre has provided a strong platform for actors, playwrights, and theatre professionals, fostering artistic excellence and building a thriving creative community. Its productions have received critical acclaim, and many of its students have gone on to establish successful careers in theatre, film, and television.

Howard Meyer is an accomplished playwright whose notable works have captured the attention of theatergoers. His play *PAINT MADE FLESH* was presented by Axial Theatre and Sotheby's NY in June 2018, directed by Cady McClain, and featured an exceptional cast, including Meredith Garretson, Stephen Grush, and David Landon. The production first debuted at The Cell Theatre in NYC following a successful workshop at Steppenwolf Theatre in Chicago. The play was later adapted into a film.

In addition to *PAINT MADE FLESH*, Meyer's latest work, *THROUPLE*, is a new comedic play featuring four characters, one set, and plenty of humor. It will have a staged reading on Thursday, February 27, 2025, at 7:00 PM at The Vineyard Theatre. The reading will feature theatre and film luminaries Rocco Sisto, Alysia Reiner, David Alan Basche, and Rose Elbay.

Meyer has received honors for several of his plays at the Eugene O'Neill National Playwrights Conference.

This is his first memoir.

www.ingramcontent.com/pod-product-compliance
Lightning Source LLC
Chambersburg PA
CBHW072126300726
48975CB00003B/950